MOON SHOWERS

Laura Phillips

A KISMET™ Romance

METEOR PUBLISHING CORPORATION
Bensalem, Pennsylvania

For Kevin, now and always.

LAURA PHILLIPS

Laura Phillips dreams of inheriting an antebellum mansion in the country. Since that isn't likely to happen, she makes do with the ranch house and large yard she shares with her husband, three children, and assorted pets.

Other books by Laura Phillips:

I have no one now. Nothing.

The rooms of the slightly faded antebellum mansion fairly bulged. Old neighbors and a few new ones from the houses that kept springing up in the vicinity of the county lake like mushrooms after a warm spring rain. Fellow teachers from the university. Students. And he'd counted twenty from the Civil War Reenactors group.

Counting helped. Concentrating on small details: the crack splitting the wall behind Mrs. Chandler's head, the scratched woodwork and faded flowers · in the carpet.

Count the flowers. Count the people and people parts, eyes, elbows, flapping lips. Don't think of the larger picture. Not yet. Twenty Reenactors. Twenty plus three was Sarah's age. Twenty plus eight was his own. And twenty years plus twenty, and maybe more after that, stretched ahead of him. If only . . .

Elbow to elbow, the well-meaning friends stood around the long table, filling plates with potato salad and fried chicken as if this were some sort of picnic. Mrs. Pierce and Mrs. Brown, from the little white

7

church down the road, had organized the buffet supper. And Old Man Neill had invited them all here after the funeral.

This was supposed to make them all feel better, but Sam just wished everyone would go away. He wished he could get out of this house. But his absence would be noticed and remarked upon, dissected and examined until they all came knocking on his door to see how he was holding up.

"There you are, son." A strong hand gripped his shoulder, halting him. "The missus and I wondered if you were doing anything for dinner Tuesday night. Margaret said she'd make a fresh cherry pie if you come."

Sam nodded, even as he scanned the room he'd been about to enter. "Of course. Have you seen Benjamin?"

The lined face crinkled thoughtfully. "Not for a while. Though if I was him, I'd lock myself upstairs in the library and drink myself into a stupor."

Sam sighed. "Not a bad idea." When the grip on his shoulder tightened, he forced a weak smile. "Don't worry, Mr. Chandler. I doubt it would help much anyway."

He walked on before the man could protest further. Finally, he made his way up the creaking stairs to the relative quiet of the second floor. For a moment, he leaned back against the cool plaster, clenching his eyes closed, gritting his teeth against a pain so deep and wrenching it was almost physical. That's when he heard the music.

Sarah's song.

It wasn't really, but he'd always called it that. Rimsky-Korsakov's *Scheherazade* had been her favorite symphony, and he learned later that she'd picked up her passion for classical music and literature from her Grandfather Benjamin.

Sam pushed away from the wall and followed the sound of the music to the end of the hall. He hesitated for an instant while the music dipped and swelled, then he pushed open the door as the sound peaked.

The old man didn't hear him at first. Benjamin Neill attacked the wallpaper with a wide, flat scraper, jabbing and prying until he'd worked a section loose. Then, with a satisfied growl, he tore off a huge strip.

"Grandpa Ben?" Sam called softly.

Sarah's grandfather didn't answer.

"Are you all right, Grandpa Ben?"

Benjamin stopped. Turning with deliberate, measured slowness, he straightened and cloaked himself with all the self-assurance Sam remembered. Even with bits of paper and plaster in his hair and on the shoulders of his somber suit, he wore his dignity like an invisible shield.

"What do you think?" he asked grimly. "I just buried my whole family. Maggie was my only child. And Sarah, little Sarah." His rheumy eyes filled, and his voice cracked at the end. "Even John. He was a good husband to my Maggie."

Sam couldn't speak. He turned to leave the man alone to exorcise his grief whatever way he chose. That bottle was sounding better and better. What did it matter if there would be hell to pay in the morning? Tonight could at least be a welcome blur.

Ben's voice stopped him before he reached the door. "They're all still here, aren't they?"

"Mostly," he answered without turning. He knew from the scratching sounds behind him that the old man had returned to demolishing the wallpaper.

"They mean well," Ben said. "Just don't tell them what I'm doing up here. Can't have them thinking I've tipped over the edge."

Sam turned, puzzled by the bitter humor in the old man's voice. "What *are* you doing?"

"Redecorating." Ben tugged another long strip of paper off the wall, stepping backwards across the room as he peeled it free.

"Now?"

"I need to work with my hands, with my back. After I get these ridiculous flowers off the wall, I'm going to strip that white paint off the woodwork. I suspect there's good walnut underneath," he said. "Here, take this for a minute." He held out the scraper.

Sam took it. "When I heard the music, I thought for a minute that Sarah wasn't—" He paused, unable to speak the words.

"Dead? I know. I was that way for awhile after we lost my Mary. Sarah's grandmother," he added for Sam's benefit. "I always hated this carpet. Think I ought to rip it out?"

Sam glanced down at the matted olive green at his feet. Dropping the scraper onto a nearby chair, he strode slowly to the back corner and moved a chair. Then he moved the side table and Mary's Tiffany lamp before kneeling on the floor.

"This looks like a good enough place to start," he said, ripping the carpet loose at the corner, then giving a mighty yank.

ONE

Seven years, she thought. After all that time, she'd finally gotten a second chance to get inside. And she didn't want to wait another minute.

"Is breaking and entering a felony in Missouri? Or is it just a misdemeanor if we don't take anything?" Kyle asked.

Hilary Neill scowled at the familiar face above the lean frame hovering close to hers. The sunshine highlighted the back of his head like a halo, burnishing red-gold highlights in his dark blond hair. But his taunting expression squelched the saint-like image. Turning, she squinted at the keyhole, ignoring the question. Kyle was just needling her for her lack of foresight, and she wasn't ready to admit he was right.

"We could come back later," he suggested after a bit.

"No, we can't," she replied. Kyle Adams, real-estate agent extraordinaire, might be satisfied with strolling around in the spongy, damp grass of the shaded yard, but not Hilary. The instant they'd driven onto Neill land, he'd started estimating how many tract houses would fit in the acres of pastures surrounding the antebellum mansion. Not Hilary. She was more interested in what was inside.

When she and Grandpa Bob came here after the funeral, there were too many people around for her to slip away and explore, even if she'd dared. She'd waited seven years to be invited back, but no invitation had come.

She twisted the nail file gently, then cursed under her breath when it broke in two. She let the pieces fall, landing on the porch planks atop her mangled American Express card.

"I told you it wouldn't work." The barely suppressed irritation in his voice grated along her nerve endings, and she wished he'd stayed in Chicago.

She should have kept her mouth shut about her impromptu trip instead of blurting out her news the minute she saw him this morning. But how was she to know there'd be another vacant seat on the plane or that he'd even consider giving up the chance to show all those high-priced houses to prospective buyers during the weekend's prime selling hours. She'd forgotten what a nose he had for an opportunity. Neill House was definitely that, as he'd so avidly pointed out for the last half-hour.

Money talks. Hilary's frown deepened. She immediately felt petty and disloyal for criticizing, even mentally, the same qualities that had drawn her to him in the first place. Ambitious and successful, he got things done. He didn't wait around for life to throw kudos in his lap. He went out and earned them.

She straightened, chewing thoughtfully on her lower lip. "Let's check that shed out back. Maybe there's another spare key somewhere. Or a ladder."

Kyle cleared his throat and cast a nervous look down the still empty driveway. "Wouldn't it be simpler to wait for the caretaker to get home, and then ask him for the key?''

Hilary stood, brushing the dust from the hem of her tailored, black wool skirt. ''The electricity is probably shut off. We won't be able to see a thing after dark.''

''Yeah? Well, if we keep this up, we're not going to see anything but the inside of the county jail.''

Hilary didn't bother to hide her annoyance. ''Please. Check the shed. I'll look in the shrubbery and around the foundation.''

''What makes you think another key exists?''

''Instinct,'' she said. ''And a working knowledge of the Neill mind.''

''You never even met Benjamin Neill,'' Kyle argued.

''I did once, although I don't suppose it counts since he didn't seem to notice me. I can't say I blame him, losing his whole family like that. Anyway, Grandpa Bob had six spare keys hidden outside. And Benjamin was his twin brother. They must have been alike in lots of ways. This might be one of them.''

''And it might not, but—'' he said, throwing up his hands in surrender. ''I know better than to argue with you when you're in one of your moods. Just one thing—''

''What now?''

''You're sure this is the right place? I wouldn't want to break into the wrong house.''

''You couldn't read the name on the mailbox? Besides, the place looks the same as last time I was here, right down to the tulips on the front lawn.''

He muttered something as he turned away, but Hilary thought it better not to ask what. Ten to one it was unflattering. She waited until he disappeared from sight before she left the porch. And then it wasn't to rummage through the bushes. Aside from the fact she wasn't dressed for it, she doubted there was another key, no matter what she'd told Kyle. Grandpa Bob and his twin brother had been opposites, according to the few stories she'd heard. If Grandpa Bob had left spare keys hidden about like Easter eggs, Great Uncle Benjamin probably had kept his one copy tucked away in his pocket, even when he slept.

She followed the flagstone path around the corner of the house, nudging the brick edging of the overgrown flower beds until she found a loose piece. The soil made a faint sucking sound as she pulled it free of the muck.

Her low heels clacked dully on the flagstones, then clicked up the steps as she returned to the front door.

Feeling a little bit like a juvenile delinquent, she pulled her arm back, preparing to fling the brick through the glass sidelight. The afternoon sunshine glimmered against the wavy glass, intensifying the rippled effect and highlighting the faint bubbles she spotted on one of the panes. Something deep inside her balked at destroying what her predecessors had painstakingly built and cared for.

Shaking her head, she lowered the brick and edged along the porch to the nearest window. She tested it, but it didn't budge, thanks to the closed latch located about even with her nose. The six panes of the lower sash appeared as old as the sidelight, as did five of the upper panes. But the one right by the lock was clear and clean, except for a few splattered raindrops that hadn't yet dried. The unpainted glazing that rimmed the glass indicated that it had recently been replaced. Apparently someone else had been here before her— and had trouble with the door, too.

Not allowing herself time for second thoughts, she raised the brick to shoulder height and bashed in one of the panels. She was knocking away the broken pieces of glass that clung to the glazing when Kyle came running around the corner.

"What happened?"

"I found a way in," she replied, handing him the brick. "Will you please put that back in the flower bed around the corner?"

Kyle groaned. "You don't have much of a future as a cat burglar. You probably set off the security system."

"There isn't one." She reached carefully through the opening she'd made and unlocked the window. The bottom sash slid smoothly upward, with none of the sticking resistance she'd expected in this grand old place.

"I'll go first," he offered, taking his jacket off and folding it over the porch rail. "I'll let you in the front door."

"Good idea," Hilary agreed. At five foot five, she was nearly a foot shorter than he. It was an easy reach for him to slip one leg over the sill and climb inside. For her, it could prove awkward at best, especially with a slim-cut skirt.

"You were wrong," he said a moment later as he unlatched the door. "The electricity's still on." He threw the door open wide, letting her pass.

Hilary's breath caught in her throat as she walked past him into the brightly lit foyer. It wasn't at all like she remembered, and the uneasy thought that she was in the wrong house crossed her mind. Then she saw the oak hall tree with the ivory and brass hardware. Carved in the wood at the top, amidst the oak leaves and acorns, was the family name—Neill. There couldn't be another like it anywhere in the country.

But the dingy carpeting and faded wallpapers were gone. The polished wood floors shone dully through the fine layer of dust that coated everything. While Kyle opened the heavy drapes, Hilary wandered from room to room, wondering how the arthritic old man she remembered had managed to transform the faded house into a museum of antebellum life. Running her hand lightly along the wood of a huge antique loom she found in a room off the kitchen, she got an eerie sense of otherworldliness, as if she'd travelled back in time. When she heard footsteps behind her, she turned, half expecting to see the ghost of one of her ancestors.

"It's a quaint old place, I'll have to admit," Kyle said. His familiar face and no-nonsense attitude dispelled any odd notions of ghosts and times long past.

Hilary nodded, although quaint wasn't the word she'd choose. It was a museum. There was no other word for it. The only things missing were the placards and the tour guides. *And the ghosts,* she thought with a whimsical chuckle.

Neill House wasn't all that large by today's standards, certainly not in the same league as some of the luxurious homes Kyle had sold back in Chicago. But it must have been quite a showplace when it was built. She could understand why Grandpa Bob had never been able to forget it.

"This is going to take longer than I expected," Hilary said, backing out of the room.

Out of habit, Sam Langford nearly turned his battered blue pickup truck onto the road snaking between the twin pillars, through the trees, and over the crest of the hill to Benjamin Neill's big house. But he caught himself at the last instant. Instead, he eased the truck a few feet past and turned in the opposite direction, into his own driveway.

Grandpa Ben's house belonged to somebody else now. The old man's brother had inherited the place when Ben died four months ago. And the last Sam heard, the inheritance was in limbo while the lawyers located the heir and tied up the loose ends.

As Sam climbed out to check the mailbox, he glanced back across the blacktop road separating his place from the Neill property. Memories of the old man had haunted him throughout the weekend. He supposed this lingering grief was only natural, considering how much time they'd spent together in the last few years when the family had dwindled down to the two of them. One really, although Ben had insisted that Sam was more Neill than those Chicago relatives who'd come for the funeral and never bothered to visit again. However, Ben hadn't done much to encourage them either. Sam really couldn't blame them for keeping their distance.

Still, it was a true Neill who'd inherited the bulk of Ben's considerable estate. In the end, blood had been thicker than the thready ties binding Sam and Ben together. In his head, he knew it was right that Ben's brother regained his boyhood home. In his heart, he felt a bit proprietorial about the house he'd helped restore.

Reaching one hand toward the mailbox, Sam scratched his bristled face with the other. Damn, but he itched, and not just beneath his fledgling beard. He suspected he didn't smell too good either, not after playing soldier in his blue wool Union uniform for three days. Re-creating the conditions of a Civil War battlefield was an interesting challenge. It brought his textbook knowledge to life and allowed him to escape himself for a few days. It also made him damned thankful he lived in the latter half of the 20th century.

A hot shower would be heaven. That's the second thing he'd do when he got home. The first would be to shed this mud-caked uniform. The rain on Friday had turned their battlefield into a marsh. The intermittent showers the rest of the weekend had assured it would stay that way. Even so, the annual muster had been a success.

A gust of wind caught at the envelopes as he pulled them from the box, and he had to step on one that fluttered to the ground and skittered toward the ditch. Something clattered behind him. Glancing over his shoulder, Sam saw the wide gate between Neill's stone pillars swing open, then bang back shut as the wind eased. The chain that was supposed to secure it hung loosely over one painted rail.

Sam stiffened. He clearly remembered latching the gate, but couldn't recall whether he'd snapped the fastener down over the chain that provided the extra security. Damn! He only hoped the cattle hadn't gotten out, too.

Crossing the blacktop, Sam checked the roadside for hoofprints. He didn't see any, but that wasn't solid evidence considering the weekend rain. There were none in the mud by the gate either. What he saw there was worse—fresh tire tracks. One set.

Returning to his truck, Sam slammed it into reverse and drove through the opened gate, stopping only long enough to latch it behind him. He spotted the cattle just over the top of the ridge, and a quick count told him all were there with one addition, a newborn, bald-faced calf.

The gate to the yard stood wide open, too, but Sam didn't bother to latch it. His attention centered on the sleek, black sedan parked in front of the house. Then he spotted the broken window.

He remembered hearing about a rash of burglaries in the suburbs last week. Had the burglars moved farther afield? Or perhaps someone had been waiting for a chance to loot the place while it was unguarded. Neill House was loaded with valuables, antiques, first editions, and odd implements he and Ben had discovered at auctions and in attics. The family silver alone would be quite a haul for the discerning thief. But that didn't account for the feeling of violation that touched Sam to his soul—as if his own home had been defiled.

He eased the truck to a halt behind the black sedan, frowning at the late-model car. A bag of groceries with a thick cluster of celery on the top sat next to the right rear window. Somehow it didn't fit the picture. Thieves drove old, battered pickups or delivery trucks to haul their ill-gotten goods away. And they didn't stop at the grocery store on the way to a heist. But this car could be stolen, too.

With that thought, Sam reached back inside the pickup for his rifle. The single-shot 1861 Springfield wouldn't be much good against armed robbers, especially loaded with the blanks he used at the reenactments. Still, the evidence indicated he probably wouldn't be facing hardened criminals. And he knew how intimidating a look down the barrel could be to a thief caught red-handed. He'd felt a quiver or two himself during a mock battle, even knowing his capturer's gun was loaded with blanks.

He took a couple of minutes to let the air out of the sedan's tires, then carefully made his way up to the porch. The front door stood wide open, but there was no sign of the intruder. A broom rested just inside the front hall, and he nearly tripped over the dustpan filled with glass shards.

Sam hesitated, puzzled. Whoever heard of a burglar who cleaned up after himself? Then he heard the voices, a man's and a woman's, drifting up from the heat register in the wide foyer. Frowning, Sam stopped to listen to the conversation carried so clearly through the antiquated ventilation system. After a moment, he heard footsteps overhead, followed by deep rumbling laughter and a loud crash from the study upstairs.

"Is this it?" the man called.

The footsteps halted, then retreated.

"No, I think that's a reproduction," the woman said. "Be careful. You're going to knock that lamp over again, and it's a genuine Tiffany, though what it's doing here I can't imagine."

"It doesn't seem to fit, does it? Hey, what's this? Good heavens, this thing must be a hundred years old. I wonder if the combination is somewhere in that old desk."

Sam stiffened at the remark. They'd found the wall safe in the study. He wondered if Ben had ever taken his suggestion and moved his wife's jewelry to the safe deposit box at the bank. Probably not. Ben's lawyer hadn't mentioned it either, although there really was no good reason for him to do so.

He clutched the rifle and started upstairs, carefully avoiding the squeaky fourth step. He'd just rounded the landing when the voices came closer. He lifted the rifle higher, prepared to fire it if necessary to frighten the burglars away.

He took the rest of the stairs two at a time. He'd almost reached the top when a slight figure rounded the corner, her arms filled with linens. He had an instant's glimpse of short brown hair and the Neill smile before she released a small, strangled cry.

A chill raced up Hilary's spine as the man leaped up the stairs, his gun pointed straight at her chest. He looked like something straight out of *Gone With The Wind*, only this wasn't Tara. The rage burning in his eyes terrified her.

She tried to scream, to call to Kyle, but her vocal chords refused to react. The man's rage changed to confusion, then fear, oddly enough. He tipped the gun aside and held a tentative hand out to her. She backed away, flinging her load of folded bedding at him.

White, crisply folded sheets hit him full in the face. He jerked backward as the folds flew open, caught on the rifle, and tangled. He teetered on the top step for an instant, arms flailing against the imprisoning cloth. The rifle fired harmlessly into the wall, then fell over the railing to the floorboards far below. He lost his tenuous footing and tumbled down the stairs, ending in a crumpled heap on the landing.

"My God! Hilary!"

Vaguely, she noted Kyle's voice, his fingertips on her shoulders. Her knees failed her, and she sank to the floor, squeezing her eyes closed. *Things like this didn't happen to her.* She'd open her eyes, and there'd be no angry ghost in a Union uniform on the stairs, just polished wood and cabbage-rose wallpaper. Then she'd come up with a good explanation for Kyle.

She blinked twice and gasped at the crumpled heap of humanity on the landing, not a ghost, but a man who might have broken his neck in that fall. Her fear faded away, replaced by concern for the stranger, however oddly dressed he might be. When he moved and groaned, she pulled out of Kyle's grasp and hurried down the steps.

"Don't move him yet," Kyle said.

But the man was already moving. Hilary held out a hand to help him. Warm, solid flesh touched hers, sending a second tingling jolt of shock through her body. This was no apparition, but a living, breathing anachronism, from the polished brass buttons of his coat to the scruffy tips of his fledgling beard.

"Sarah?" he muttered. His dazed eyes mirrored her own shock. They gradually focused on her face, then narrowed with suspicion and finally relief. "No, thank God."

"Are you all right?" she asked. She realized what a stupid question it was when she saw the blood oozing from a cut at his temple. She reached out a tentative hand to help him.

"Git," he said, back to his ferocious self.

"What?"

"Just get out of here. Don't take anything, and I won't press charges," the man said, locking solid fingers around her wrist in an iron grasp. Hilary tried to jerk away, then caught a glimpse of pain mixed with the anger in his chocolate brown eyes.

"Let go of her," Kyle demanded. When the man didn't obey, Kyle reached across and tried to loosen his grip. A well-placed boot sent him sprawling against the solid, wood rail.

That's when Hilary aimed her foot for the spot where her Grandpa Bob had said it would do the most damage. The man twisted, and the blow glanced off his hip. A blood-curdling yell filled the air like a battle cry as he rolled away to the far side of the small landing.

Startled, Hilary fell back against the wall, her mouth gaping open. Kyle seemed similarly stunned.

"All right, now that I have your attention," the man said. "Take whatever you want. Just leave me alone. Nothing in the damn house is worth this." He pushed himself to his feet, wincing and holding his arm gingerly at his side. He limped down the stairs and reached for the broken stock of his rifle, groaning as he bent over.

When Kyle started to follow, Hilary stopped him with a staying hand.

"Go upstairs and call the sheriff," Kyle said.

The man straightened. "By all means," he said and reeled off the number. He sidestepped to retrieve the rest of the rifle.

Hilary tilted her head, staring at the battered intruder. "Who are you?"

One dark brow lifted, then he winced and touched a

finger to his temple. "Well now, that depends. A while ago I thought I was your worst nightmare. Turns out, you're mine."

As she watched him limp out, Hilary's eyes widened in confusion. What in heaven's name was going on here?

"Kyle?"

"I think maybe we need the guys with the white coats more than we need the sheriff," he commented, taking her arm. "Let's go see what he's up to now."

By the time they reached the front porch, the man was halfway to a battered pickup truck. He halted, then turned around and surveyed the two of them with mocking eyes. "Sorry about your tires. I guess a quick getaway is out of the question."

"A quick getaway?" Kyle's hand tightened on Hilary's arm. "Damn it, I told you we should have waited for the caretaker. Now we're stuck with flat tires and a lunatic."

Hilary shrugged out of his grip and stepped beyond him into the bright sunlight on the front walk. "Who are you?" she repeated, punctuating each word with a stamped footstep in the intruder's direction. She didn't stop walking, either, until she was practically nose to nose with him.

"Damn, but you're the pushiest burglar I ever heard of," he muttered.

Hilary sputtered, then poked a pointed nail dead center in the man's chest. "I have a right to be here. You don't. Explain yourself."

For a moment he didn't say anything. Then the corner of his frown twitched as if he were having a hard time keeping it in place.

"Whatever you say, lady." When he started to turn away, Hilary stopped him. The muscles of his arm tightened beneath her fingers, and she dropped her hand instantly.

"The house is mine. I found out late last night," she insisted as his skeptical gaze lifted to meet hers.

"And I'm Robert E. Lee," the man replied, slipping into a slow Southern drawl as easily as a duck into water. "Benjamin Neill left this place to his brother, who was gallivanting around the world with some young girl, last anyone heard."

"Vacationing. And that young girl was a forty-five-year-old registered nurse."

"Whatever."

"He died in London two months ago." Hilary had said it so many times that it came out smoothly, with barely a hint of emotion. But she must have revealed something because his faint frown lines softened, rearranging themselves into a mask of sympathy.

"My God, you are telling the truth," he whispered.

Hilary hesitated. His sudden about-face unnerved her. "What changed your mind?"

"Your eyes. I see it now. Ben would get that look sometimes when he talked about his family, all pent-up sadness hiding behind a composed face. You have Ben's eyes, and your hair, it reminds me of—never mind. It wasn't my imagination after all, not completely." He seemed heartened by that knowledge, which further confused her. "The eyes had me fooled there for a minute. I was looking for brown, not gray like Ben's."

"What does that have to do with—"

"So, you're the Neill heir, huh? That explains the resemblance, though you're not what I expected."

"Really? Well, now it's your turn," she said with a challenging stare. The silent battle of wills lasted only an instant before he sighed, conceding to her stubbornness.

"I promised Ben I'd keep an eye on the place while he was in the hospital. Guess I got in the habit," he said, in a reluctant tone. The frown gave way to a slightly crooked smile. "I live across the road."

Across the road? Hilary squinted, taking in the angry glints lingering in eyes that had turned tawny in the sunlight. Again, a vague sense of familiarity teased her senses and she concentrated on remembering what she'd learned about the Missouri branch of the family during that brief visit with Grandpa Bob. They'd come for the funeral when three Neills had been laid to rest after a tragic explosion caused by a leaking gas valve. A mental picture of a grieving young man teased her, but it didn't quite match the scruffy creature before her. Or did it? She imagined him without the beard in a solemn black suit.

"You live in the foreman's house? You're Samuel Langford," she added after his confirming nod.

"You know this nut?" Kyle's voice boomed in her ear. Hilary glanced in surprise over her shoulder. She hadn't heard him come up behind her. She'd been too busy with the puzzle of their stubble-bearded intruder.

"Yes," she confirmed, turning back around. "We met several years ago."

Both of Sam's dark brows lifted, questioning.

"At the funeral," she said, then wished she'd kept her mouth shut when a shadow crossed his expression. *His wife's funeral.* "I doubt you'd remember. I didn't recognize you myself until just this minute. You've—umm—changed a bit," she said, letting her gaze travel down the length of the mussed, period uniform to the mud-encrusted boots, then back to his stubbled face.

A faint smile crossed his lips, though his expression remained wary. "I was on the way home from the re-enactment of a Civil War battle. It's a hobby of mine, one Ben Neill used to share." He took a step back and bowed low, taking Hilary's hand and raising it to his lips in a courtly gesture that seemed as out of tune with his grubby image as a harp at a fiddling contest. "You have the advantage of me, ma'am. I still cannot believe we've met, or I would surely be able to recall the name that matches your lovely face. What relation are you to dear old Ben?"

She blinked in surprise, then the words gushed out of her mouth in a nervous rush. "I'm Hilary Neill, Benjamin Neill's great-niece. I was with Grandpa Bob, Ben's brother, when we met."

"Ah, the good little granddaughter with the pony-tail," he said, scrunching his brows as if recalling a vague memory. "I suppose you've come to take a look at the old family home. Sorry I wasn't around to give you the key."

"You're the caretaker?" Kyle asked, his tone skeptical.

Sam shrugged. "Something like that. If you'll pardon my asking, how did you come to be the new owner? As I understood it, the place goes to the county historical society if Ben's brother can't inherit."

She stiffened. "He inherited it, all right. Then he died shortly after Uncle Benjamin. I suppose that complicated things. But believe this, I am the heir." The lump of emotion in her throat surprised her. She thought she'd dealt with the grief and put it behind her. She had. It was only the after effect of all the commotion that made her vulnerable. That and the warm compassion that sprang up so unexpectedly in Samuel's eyes.

"Sorry," he said, reaching for her hand. "It's hard losing the people you love."

She shook her head. "It was his time." Grandpa Bob had kept telling her that, over and over until he slipped into the coma. And somehow, he'd made her believe it.

Sam nodded. "Ben's, too. I still miss him, though."

She believed him. The truth trembled in the gravelly pitch of his voice, in the liquid brown eyes that captured hers. A chill chased goose bumps up her arm from the warmth of his hand to the sleeve where Kyle's hand tightened on her arm.

She cleared her throat, sensing Kyle's displeasure. "Sam, this is Kyle Adams, my fiancé."

Sam's warm look faltered, and his touch became impersonal. "Congratulations, Mr. Adams," he said. "Or should I say condolences. I hope you survive long enough to marry her. Or does she only push strangers down the stairs?"

"I didn't push you. I thought you were . . ." Her voice trailed off. She thought he was what? A ghost?

"And I thought you were a burglar," he replied with the beginnings of a laugh.

Unfortunately, Kyle didn't see the humor. "Most people would have called the police and left it at that."

"I'm not most people," Sam said, turning back toward the truck. "Sorry about your tires. I'll send someone over with an air tank."

A moment later he was gone, leaving Hilary alone with a vaguely unsettled feeling and a very irritated fiancé.

TWO

Sam shuffled through the papers on his desk, hunting for a red pen that hadn't dried up. He couldn't contain the grunt of displeasure when he came across the letter, the one informing him that as a neighboring property owner, he had a right to voice his opinion on Hilary Neill's rezoning request. That was one right he intended to exercise the first chance he got. He stuck the envelope up on the bulletin board, impaling it with a vicious stab of the thumbtack.

That's what he thought of her plan. It was bad enough that she intended to turn Neill Farm into a subdivision. But to convert the house itself into a combination gas station and convenience store—that was too much. That house was in the National Register of Historic Places. He wondered if she knew that, or if it meant anything to her.

It must not, or she wouldn't have instigated this idiocy.

Hilary Neill *was* his worst nightmare. At first sight, she'd reminded him of his gentle Sarah, with her short hair swirled atop her head. Then he'd glimpsed Hilary's storm-cloud gray eyes, the instant before she'd sent him tumbling down the stairs.

After six weeks, his bruises had healed. But just thinking about the woman made his back ache. It made other parts of him ache, too. He wouldn't let himself think about that, though, because it didn't make sense.

Sharp-tongued number crunchers weren't his type. He liked his women pleasant and a little bit dreamy.

So, he wouldn't remember her softness as she spoke of her grandfather, or the way her hand had quivered in his. He dismissed the jolt of feeling that left him breathless when she'd touched him, even when he was lying in pain on the landing. Chemistry wasn't reason enough for him to overlook certain facts. She was engaged to be married, and from the looks of things she and that slick Chicago fiancé deserved one another.

In the meantime . . . well, in the meantime, he had papers to grade. Judging from the pile on his desk, it would be a long weekend. He wished, not for the first time, that he hadn't agreed to teach this summer class.

He was three hours into the stack of research papers when tires crunched in the gravel out front. Peering out the side window, he saw the vague outline of a car in the moonless night. Sam groaned as the dome light revealed the identity of the driver. Hilary Neill. Alone.

Through the slit between the mini-blinds, he watched her climb out, revealing a quick flash of thigh before she stood and her skirt slid down to cover her legs. Then she stepped out of sight behind the shrubbery.

Damn. This he didn't need. Or maybe he did, he thought as the rezoning notice drew his gaze. Here was his chance to speak his mind before things got out of hand, before the neighborhood had to resort to legal measures to stop her. A low hum of anticipation zipped through his veins.

He opened the door before she had a chance to knock.

Hilary took a backward step at the sight of the clean-shaven stranger. Then she recognized Sam, minus the stubble and grime. Tonight he looked more like that sad man she'd met years ago at the funeral. He seemed angry, and she wondered whether he'd been asleep. Or maybe he had company, and she'd disturbed them.

"Lose your key?" His voice dripped sarcasm.

Coming here was a mistake, Hilary decided as she took in the subtle hostility in his stance.

She recovered quickly from the shock of his sudden appearance and pasted a friendly smile on her face. Might as well try to be pleasant, even if their last meeting had left a bad taste in her mouth—his, too, judging from his expression. Besides, she needed his help.

"I have them, thank you. And thank you again for sending your friend over with them. It's a shame your air compressor was on the blink. It took me and Kyle forever with that hand pump," she said, in a deceptively sweet tone that sickened even her. Before her smile could slip, she looked away, slapping at a mosquito.

"Come inside," he said, holding the screen wide.

She stepped past him into the central hall, then wished she'd stayed where she was, mosquitoes be damned. It was dark there, even darker than on the front porch where a single yellow bulb shone dimly through a dusty globe. The house was quiet—too quiet. She was alone with him. To her relief, he flicked a switch, throwing the entry hall into vivid light. She glanced around, noting the similarities between this house and the one she'd just left. The foreman's place was much smaller, but almost as old, judging from the wear on the polished floorboards. The rail posts matched those in the big house, as did the dark, paneled doors.

"So, what brings you here at this hour?" Sam asked as he latched the screen.

"The water appears to be shut off. I found the valve, but I can't budge it. I wondered if I might borrow a wrench. Or perhaps you could tell me where Uncle Ben kept his."

His eyes swept the length of her, lingering on the mustard silk blouse and then the tweed, slit skirt. "Don't you think you're a little overdressed for plumbing work?"

"I'd only planned to turn the water on, not replumb the house," she replied, matching his sarcasm with her own. "Never mind. If you don't want to help, just say so. I'll take a bath in the cattle trough."

His amusement surprised her. "You might have to," he replied. "Of course, if you'd checked ahead of time, you'd know that I had to shut the water off two days ago. You have a leak. A very big one. Or didn't you notice the new pond in the front yard?"

"It's dark, Mr. Langford," she reminded him. "No moon. No stars. I had to find the keyhole by touch."

"Where's your other half? Not up there banging the pipes, I hope."

"If you're referring to Kyle, he's still in Chicago. He couldn't get away this weekend." *Good job, Hilary,* she berated herself when Sam's chin tilted thoughtfully upwards. She half expected a snide, sexist remark or a proposition, judging from the sudden warmth in his gaze. Instead, he nodded and offered her a cup of coffee.

"No, thanks," she said. "I'd better be going. I still need to make a couple of phone calls."

"Your fiancé?"

She nodded. "And someone from the office. I came

straight from New York." She didn't add that the day had been as unpleasant as it had been long. Actually, she dreaded both the calls. She had only bad news to report. She wanted to ask where Uncle Ben had kept his liquor, particularly the Scotch, then decided that might give the wrong impression. Never mind, she'd find it on her own or do without.

Her uncertainty must have shown because Sam moved past her and switched on the overhead light in the next room. "Suit yourself. We can talk now or tomorrow. But we are going to talk about a few things before you leave this time."

"Such as?"

"Neill House. People around here are pretty concerned about what you plan to do with it," he said, pausing in the doorway.

Her gaze narrowed as he disappeared into the next room. He sounded like a man with a purpose, though she was relieved to note that purpose didn't seem to be seduction. His was a calm and collected anger, one she could reason with if she only knew its source. Maybe he resented her inheriting Uncle Ben's place and the changes that were certain to follow. Some people were like that. Or maybe he'd wanted it for himself.

Hilary hesitated, then followed him down the wide hall past a pair of threadbare chairs and a cluttered, dusty chest to the tiny kitchen at the back of the house. She'd nearly reached the doorway when a group of photographs on the wall above the chest caught her eye. For a moment, she saw herself staring back at her from the studio portrait at the center. Then she noticed the longer hair, the brown eyes instead of gray, and faint differences in the shape of the face and the slender fingertips that caressed the strand of pearls around the woman's neck. Hilary knew instinctively that the woman was Sarah, her second cousin and Sam's dead wife.

She tucked the image away in the corner of her mind and entered the kitchen.

"I made a fresh pot a little while ago," he said as she entered the room. "It helps keep me awake while I wade through freshman research papers."

"You're a teacher?"

"That's about all you can do with a Ph.D. in American history. The Civil War is my specialty."

Her brows arched in surprise. "That explains the costume. I guess you take your history seriously."

His sharp look relaxed after a moment when he saw she wasn't mocking him, and he shrugged lightly. "Seriously enough. You should try it sometime. Reenactment gives you a better perspective on the past. It also makes you appreciate the amenities of the present a lot more."

"I'll bet," she replied, thinking of his grubby, unshaven state the last time they had met. "Which brings us back to the immediate problem. I suppose I should ask you to recommend a plumber," she said as he handed her a cup. "What are the chances of getting someone out here tomorrow?"

"Not good."

"I was afraid of that," she said. "Where is the leak? I only tried the bathrooms and the kitchen. I didn't check any of the outdoor faucets." She took the chair he indicated and sipped the bitter brew, trying not to scowl. Those papers must be worse than she'd imagined, if he needed industrial-strength caffeine to keep him awake.

"Your leak is someplace between the back porch and the pump shed. The hydrants work, except for the one on the west side of the house by the rose bushes. At least you'll be able to get water, if you don't mind carrying it.''

"I'll manage," she said. "Grandpa Bob and I used to camp a lot. Running water is a minor detail."

"Glad you see it that way. You brought other clothes?"

She shrugged. "I can pick something up tomorrow. I have business to attend to."

"With the attorneys?" His lips hardened into an uncompromising line, and she wondered why that bothered him. Watching him covertly over the rim of her cup, she took another sip and considered her next words.

"Among other things," she finally said. "I need to decide what to do with this place."

"I thought that had already been decided."

"Not yet. I'm still considering my options."

"Come off of it, Ms. Neill. I got the notice in the mail two days ago. So you can stop pretending."

"What are you talking about?"

He cast her a disbelieving look, then shoved his chair back and stalked into the other room. A moment later, he dropped an envelope on the table in front of her.

"Don't tell me you didn't know anything about that."

She picked up the envelope and studied it. With a questioning glance at him, she pulled out the letter and perused it. As she read, a cold spot of anger grew inside, although she kept her features carefully blank. It seemed that Kyle had done more than check out the local real estate market. And he'd had the nerve to call her impetuous.

"Would you mind if I borrowed this, just for tomorrow?" she asked.

He leaned closer, studying her. "Don't you have your own copy?"

"Would I borrow yours if I did?"

"You might."

Hilary smiled cooly. "I'm not interested in those kinds of games. They're manipulative and unnecessary. Now, I think I'd better leave." She found he stood so close to her in the cramped kitchen that she couldn't get out of her chair, though, without bumping into him.

"The phone calls," he said, not moving.

"It's been a long day," she replied with a pointed look. But he didn't take the hint. Instead, he leaned even closer, tilting her chin. His touch unnerved her. She stilled, waiting to see what he'd do next.

"You didn't know, did you?" he asked, his voice soft with uncertainty.

He must have seen the truth in her eyes because he straightened before she could answer. "Hilary Neill, I don't know what to make of you," he said backing away to give her room to stand.

She slipped past him to the door, pretending a nonchalance she was far from feeling. "I'll talk to you again tomorrow" was all she said.

"And the rezoning?"

She turned for a brief instant. "This is one of the options we discussed. As I said before, I haven't made a decision yet. Somebody jumped the gun."

To her relief, he seemed to believe her. She told herself it shouldn't matter. No, it should, she reasoned. He was a neighbor. The last thing she needed was the neighborhood aligned against her in whatever she decided to do with the place.

"What else are you considering?" he asked.

She shrugged. "I'd rather not be any more specific than that. I imagine there's already enough speculation burning the telephone wires around here. I'll let you know when I get a little closer to the answer," she promised. She owed him that much at least, since he was the closest neighbor. And he was family, in a distant sort of way, having once been married to Uncle Ben's granddaughter.

"Why not use it for a weekend getaway?" he suggested.

"Mr. Langford, perhaps you've been misled about the extent of my wealth. Frankly, I can't afford it. I make a good living, but not that good. I'm just an accountant, and my job isn't all that secure right now," she said, then wished she hadn't let the last bit of information slip.

"Ben wasn't a pauper."

She shook her head. "No, he left a good amount of money for the upkeep. But a place like this could burn up the trust fund in a few years. My life is in Chicago. And I'm not extravagant enough to keep an antebellum mansion for a vacation house. If I keep Neill House, it has to pay its way somehow."

"You can't sell it," he said. "I know there's a deed restriction."

"Right. The house has to stay in the family until it falls down or the family dies out. But if you know about the deed restriction, you'll also know that most of the land *can* be sold."

He nodded. "I know. But it would be a shame to break the place up any more."

She couldn't resist a jibe of her own. "You didn't mind when Ben deeded this house and twenty-five acres to you."

Sam's expression hardened. "It was a wedding present."

Hilary swallowed uncomfortably and stared out into the night. "Sorry. I can't seem to keep my foot out of my mouth these days. Tell me? Does Missouri have that effect on anyone else?"

She heard him walk up beside her and braved a quick

look. The anger had eased from his face, replaced by an unreadable expression.

"Come on," he suggested. "I'll see you home."

"It isn't necessary," she insisted, preceding him out the door.

"There've been a few break-ins lately," he reminded her. "I wouldn't want you to walk in on a couple of looters."

She tried not to smile. "Like you thought we were," she said, reminding him of their inauspicious meeting.

He chuckled. "I won't hold that against you."

"Likewise. It's good to know somebody's watching over the place when I'm not here," she said.

He halted. "I do that for Ben," he said. "Because I respect who he was and what he believed in. Don't ever think otherwise."

She didn't doubt that. No monthly stipend bought that kind of devotion or the depth of emotion that vibrated in his voice. She couldn't think of anything to say that wouldn't sound patronizing or just plain stupid. She climbed behind the wheel without another word.

"I'll walk back. It'll wake me up enough to get through a few more papers tonight," he said, climbing into the passenger side of the rental car.

Nodding, she stuffed the rezoning notice into her purse, then started the car and backed out of the drive. They didn't bother to shut the gates now that the cattle had been sold. She suspected the farmer would turn a tidy profit almost immediately, but she really didn't mind letting them go for a below-market price. It was one less thing to worry about. And the sale had decreased Sam's caretaker duties, for which she was grateful. She didn't like being beholden to the man, no matter what his reasons for continuing in the job. Besides, it appeared they'd wind up on opposite sides regarding the future of Neill House.

Hilary parked behind the house this time, and they entered through the big, screened porch. Before going any farther, he showed her the switches for the lights mounted on the porch wall, on the shed, and back by the big, red barn.

"Thanks," she said. "I hadn't gotten around to finding them yet."

He started to speak when the phone rang.

"That's probably Kyle. Or my mother," she said, heading on into the kitchen. She heard Sam murmur something behind her as she picked up the receiver and spoke into it. But when she leaned out to peer around the corner, he was gone.

"Hilary, are you there?"

"Yes, Kyle," she said. "I was just saying good-bye to the caretaker."

"You let that nut into the house at this hour?"

"The water's been shut off. Plumbing problems. Looks like I'll be roughing it this weekend."

While Kyle voiced his misgivings, she kicked off the dark leather pumps and wriggled her toes. It felt good to get the shoes off. A quick hop seated her on the counter, her feet dangling in midair. That felt even better.

"Look, I'm not going to a motel, and I'm not coming home early just because the water is turned off," she finally said to shut off the tirade.

"But I miss you," he said, his voice going whiskey rough.

Hilary remained silent, unmoved in her anger. She cradled the phone on her shoulder, and tugged at the elastic top of her pantyhose. They had gotten increasingly uncomfortable as the day wore on, and she decided not to buy that brand again.

"Hilary? Are you still there?"

"Kyle, how much checking have you done on the real estate market down here?"

"Quite a bit, actually. I want to go through all that with you when you get home."

She drew a deep breath before speaking. "Sam Langford got a rezoning notice in the mail this week. I felt like a fool when he showed it to me. I had no idea you'd take it this far without even consulting me."

"It's only a preliminary hearing, sort of a testing of the waters," Kyle replied, sounding irritated. "That's one of the things I wanted to talk to you about."

"Why bother now?" she replied, her anger rising again. "It appears that you've already got the ball rolling quite well without me."

"Don't you think you're overreacting a little bit?"

"No, I don't think so."

"I'm sure that once I lay it all out for you and explain your options, you'll agree with me. If we can get the rezoning, we'll make a bundle."

"We?" Her hand went to the receiver, gripping it tightly.

"You know what I mean."

"No, I don't. Please explain it to me."

His sigh was audible. "Look, you're tired and grumpy. Let's talk about this in the morning when you're in a better mood."

"You should have consulted me first. It is my name on the deed."

"I tried, sweetheart. But you've been in New York or London for most of the month. I had to move fast to get it on the agenda. And you didn't return my calls."

"I was home last weekend."

"It slipped my mind. I had that closing on the lake house, and then the offer on this office complex. I wasn't trying to hide anything or sneak anything past you. I couldn't do that. As you pointed out, you're the owner. Not me.''

Hilary bit her lip. He sounded so sincere, and she suddenly felt guilty. And that made her angry all over again.

"You're right. I'm tired." She didn't want to argue anymore tonight. She couldn't change what he'd done. She'd just have to figure out her next step.

"Of course, sweetheart," Kyle soothed. "I'll talk to you tomorrow. Night, love." The line clicked, then buzzed before she could respond.

She stared at the receiver for a moment, perplexed by her fiancé's hurried good-bye. Maybe she had over-reacted. She'd asked him to check out a few things, and she had been pretty inaccessible, what with settling Grandpa's estate and all the problems at work. Slowly, she hung up the receiver on the wall behind her, frown-ing as she remembered this morning's announcement at Collins, Inc.

The senior partner had sold out to a large holding company. The rumors indicated that her department probably would be cut to avoid duplication when the companies merged. There might be a spot for her else-where, but, then again, she might end up job hunting instead.

Since neither Grandpa Bob's nor Uncle Ben's estates was completely settled, she wasn't sure where her per-sonal finances stood either. She knew she was moder-ately well-off, but the very vagueness of that bothered her.

She probably should call Kyle and apologize in the morning—right after she reminded him that he had overstepped his bounds this time. She'd chewed at him like a shrew on the phone tonight. He deserved it, though. He'd gone too far.

Still muttering to herself, she tugged again at the

pantyhose and hopped abruptly to the floor. She rolled the stocking down her right leg and stepped out of it. She was halfway down the left leg with the hose when the porch door slammed.

Hilary gasped, staring with surprise at Sam's unexpected appearance. He'd stopped suddenly, just inside the kitchen, sloshing water from both buckets he carried. He stood there, watching her with warm interest, completely unnerving her. Again, she felt a shock, a warmth so elemental it touched her soul. A recognition. For a moment, she couldn't move. Then she pulled the stocking off her foot and straightened, smoothing her skirt in jerky motions.

"I thought you were gone," she said, choking out the words.

"Apparently." His voice was as harsh as her breathing. It sent tingles up her arms, then down her spine, as if he'd touched her. She felt her nipples harden beneath her thin blouse and wished she'd worn a padded bra instead of the thin, comfortable one that revealed too much just now. She only hoped he didn't notice.

His eyes dipped, then met hers again, deepening in color until they seemed almost black. He set both buckets down.

"You're wet," she whispered.

"It's a start." He turned away, striding quickly out of the room.

"What?" she called after him. Was he not making sense, or was she completely befuddled?

He paused at the screen door, fiddling with the latch. When he turned back, his eyes melted something inside her. Dark and liquid desire smoldered there.

"It's a start on a cold shower, Hilary Neill," he repeated in a low voice. And then he was gone.

THREE

Maybe he won't be home.

That would only postpone the inevitable, but Hilary couldn't help hoping. Then she could just tuck his copy of the rezoning notice in the screen door, along with a brief note. She wouldn't have to talk to him. And she wouldn't have to explain why she only postponed the hearing, not cancelled it.

She wouldn't have to wonder, either, what he meant by his parting remark last night. She'd practically done a striptease in Ben's kitchen, unaware that she had an audience. That embarrassed her, but embarrassment wasn't what made her flush warm all over as she remembered. She'd glimpsed raw desire, and her body had responded with an answering heat that had kept her awake and restless for hours afterward. She was afraid to consider what might have happened if he'd actually touched her. She might not have objected. But he hadn't. He'd walked away.

Yet he'd left her feeling alive and desirable. And that was no way for an engaged woman to feel, not when someone besides her fiancé made it happen.

Cresting the hill, she slowed the rental car and watched for the break in the trees that signaled the two driveways, one leading to Uncle Ben's place and the opposite ending at Sam's.

The fates weren't smiling on her.

He was there, all right. Or at least his truck was. A second later, she spotted him high on a ladder painting the trim around a second-story window. Sweat gleamed on his bare legs and shoulders where a faint sunburn showed. He looked around as her car drew closer, then started to climb down as she turned onto the gravel drive. By the time she parked and got out, he was near the bottom of the ladder.

"Finished your business?" he called.

"For now," she answered, leaning against the car while he set the brush and paint can down. She could smell the paint fumes, and as he drew nearer, the salty scent of sun-warmed skin and sweat. She couldn't read his expression behind the dark sunglasses, but his lips curved into a smile as he stopped close to her.

"I just wanted to drop this off," she said, handing over the envelope containing the rezoning notice. "Not that it matters much anymore. I've asked the attorney to postpone the hearing. You should get a letter next week."

He considered for a moment, tapping the envelope against a paint-smeared palm. "Postponed, not cancelled? I guess this means you're going ahead with the subdivision."

Hilary sighed. She'd known he'd react this way. "It means that I'm keeping my options open. I can't do anything until both estates clear probate, probably that shouldn't be much longer. Then I'll know exactly how much is left once all the taxes are paid. It affects how much I can afford to do."

Sam nodded, seeming satisfied for the moment. "I

guess that makes sense. And, in the meantime, you could give me a chance to talk you out of anything foolish.''

Her smile mocked him. ''Your definition or mine?''

''Ben's,'' he said, disconcerting her for a moment.

''I should have seen that one coming,'' she replied, crossing her arms over her chest. It bothered her that she hadn't. ''You're very sure of yourself, aren't you, Dr. Langford?'' she continued, suspecting her use of his academic title would rankle.

He thinned his lips in response.

''Since you two had so much in common, and you know so much about his wishes, why did I inherit? Why not you?'' She knew her frustration showed, but she no longer cared. Kyle always told her she didn't play her cards close enough to the vest. But damn it, she didn't like dealing in half-truths, omissions, and sleights of hand. She preferred the direct route.

''He left it to his brother,'' Sam reminded her. ''Since your grandfather grew up here, the place must have meant something to him, even if he seldom visited.''

Hilary sighed. He was right. She'd grown up listening to Grandpa Bob's stories about his and Great Uncle Ben's escapades, many of which were hopelessly exaggerated. She wondered, not for the first time, what had driven the wedge between them so deeply that it had taken Ben's family tragedy to put them on speaking terms. And even that hadn't brought them close. Ben should have leaned on Grandpa, let his brother help him heal. That's what families were for.

''Before Ben went to the hospital that last time, he gave me his diaries,'' Sam said. ''I think he must have known he wouldn't be coming home. Maybe if you read them, you'd understand him better. It might help you reach your decision.''

She considered, then discarded the idea. "Maybe sometime, when everything settles down a little bit."

"I could get them now," he offered.

She shook her head. "I'm leaving tomorrow morning. I have a lot to do before then. And it's not just the estate," she continued as he frowned his irritation. "My job's pretty hectic right now. It'll settle down in a few weeks." And that, she added silently, might be the understatement of the year.

"Another time," he suggested. "Meanwhile, you could give yourself a break and have dinner with me."

Hilary's eyes darted to his. "In case you're keeping score on how many times you can catch me off-guard, that's your second hit. It's not as strong as the scare on the stairs, but it's definitely a surprise."

"It's the third hit," he corrected her, touching her cheek. And his low chuckle reminded her just what incident she'd forgotten to count. Her stomach felt like a cluster of fluttering butterflies as she remembered how he'd watched her last night.

"I have other plans," she replied, reaching for the car door handle.

His hand closed over hers, stopping her. "I shouldn't have said that," he said. "I apologize."

"Accepted," she replied, refusing to look at him. "Now, I really have to go."

"Look, there's a potluck dinner at the church. There'll be close to a hundred people there. Anybody's welcome."

"Even me?"

"It'll be a good opportunity for you to get to know some of your neighbors. It would also go a long way toward mending the fences over this rezoning thing of yours."

Hilary hesitated, and he dropped his hand and

stepped back. "And I promise to stop baiting you," he added.

"You have a point about the rezoning, but I've already made plans."

"Your fiancé's joining you?"

"No. But I have a few things to do. Odds and ends. You know, that sort of thing."

She refused to look at him, a fact that didn't escape Sam's notice. He wondered why she'd suddenly become so evasive.

"You're going anyway, aren't you?"

He nodded. "Of course. I haven't missed it in five, no six years."

"How long will you be gone, in case I run across something I need to ask you about? Or maybe I could call you later, after I finish—what I need to do—if I have any questions about Uncle Ben's things."

He stared at her as she drew circles in the gravel with her shoe. A dull flush crept up her face.

"The supper starts at seven, and things usually taper off sometime after midnight."

"Perfect," she muttered, flashing a look of mixed relief and delight.

Perfect for what? He wondered why she would be pleased that he would be gone for hours. He thought then of the single strand of pearls Ben had given Sarah on their wedding day. They were hidden away in a drawer with a few other mementos of his wife. Could Hilary have found out about them and thought they belonged with the estate? The attorney had questioned him about them. Maybe he'd mentioned them to her.

No. Of course not. Hilary Neill was too forthright for such subterfuge. She would have asked him outright, wouldn't she? Something else was bothering her.

"I could leave you the number over there, in case you have any problems," he offered. *And perhaps call before I leave so I don't interrupt something you're trying to hide.* He dismissed the sarcastic thought.

He noticed a twinkle of mischief in her answering grin. The woman was definitely up to no good. "That would be great," she said.

A niggling sense of unease pervaded him as she climbed into her car, almost bouncing with suppressed excitement. Hours later, as he polished off a plate of smoky-tasting barbecued pork, the seed of doubt in his mind had grown to prize-winning pumpkin size. He disposed of his smeared plate and utensils, made his excuses to his host, and headed back toward home.

Not a blade of grass appeared out of place at his house, but that was no more than he'd expected. The lights, the doors, all the latches were just as he'd left them. As he let himself inside, he remembered the pearl necklace again. It really did belong with the Neill estate. He had no real right to it or need of it anymore. And it was time, too, that he cleaned out that room upstairs. After Sarah's death, he'd moved down the hall, finding it impossible to rest in their old room when surrounded by his memories. He'd given away her clothes, stored the photographs, and emptied the room of her presence. But the memories remained.

As the weeks passed into months, and then years, the room had ceased to haunt him. Instead, he'd turned it into a storage space for everything he'd been too busy to carry to the attic. He ought to clean it out before it became a fire hazard. He could start tomorrow. Tonight, he'd sit back, drink a beer, and maybe watch television. And wonder some more what that woman was doing alone in the big house across the road.

Whatever she was up to had nothing to do with him, he told himself. Even if she was digging up the backyard, hunting for buried treasure, it was no concern of his. There was no reason for him to even think about her.

But he did.

Slumping on the bottom step in the darkness of the entry hall, he felt the faint stirrings of excitement as he remembered the curve of her lips, the Neill chin and the Neill eyes, then the tantalizing glimpse of pale, sleek thighs before she'd tugged her skirt into place. No woman had teased his senses like this for years, not for seven long, lonely years.

He tried to tell himself that she simply reminded him of Sarah. But the only resemblance between his quiet, dreamy Sarah and Hilary was the color of their hair and their vaguely heart-shaped faces. Where Sarah had been seductively curved, Hilary was more subtly rounded.

Hilary was a shark in the world of corporate finance. Sarah couldn't balance a checkbook. Hilary was everything that Sarah wasn't and nothing that Sarah was. Sam couldn't imagine why he was attracted to her. He must be suffering from some sort of delayed deprivation.

Yet, for an instant when they'd met, and again this evening, he'd sensed a window of vulnerability. The storm-cloud gray eyes had misted, and he'd been touched to the core. She was a puzzle.

Leaving the lights as they were, he slipped out the front door and looked toward Ben's place. The gate was still open, so he had no idea whether Hilary was there or was attending to her mischief elsewhere. However, he had to know what had made her eyes light up so brilliantly this afternoon.

Keeping to the pasture, he followed Ben's drive until he could see the house. A dim glow of light showed through the study window upstairs, but otherwise the house was dark. And the second gate was closed, although he couldn't think why since the cattle were gone now.

Drawing closer, he frowned at the hand-written sign hanging near the latch. "Honk, please," it said.

I guess she doesn't want any surprises, he thought, chuckling. *Anybody with a nickel's worth of sense would have taken the cowbells from the kitchen wall and hung them over the gate for an early warning system. She'd probably install iron gates and a buzzer if she moved here permanently. But she wasn't going to move here,* he reminded himself. She'd made that abundantly clear.

Slipping nimbly between the fence rails, he struck out for the house, keeping to the trees. He spotted her car parked by the shed. Nothing stirred near the house, and he started across the lawn. A slam of the back door made him leap behind a snowball bush.

Hilary's voice drifted through the stillness, barely louder than the chirp of the crickets and the distant croaking of bullfrogs. She hadn't turned on the porch light, but the rising moon shone brightly enough for him to follow her shadowy movements around the cluster of forsythia bushes to the oak tree opposite the rose garden.

Creeping closer, he tried to see who else was there, who she was talking to. Then something caught at his toe, tripping him and tangling around his ankle.

Biting back a growl, he worked himself free of the twisted garden hose that had ensnared him. Still warm from the sun's heat, it must have lain there most of the day. He started to roll it up out of habit, then dropped it. She left it out. She could put it away.

His irritation doubled as his eyes picked out the snaking trail of several lengths of hose strung across the yard. She'd gotten out every foot of hose on the place. Deciding the situation was growing stranger by the minute, he crept still closer and tried to make out her words. He was about twenty feet away when he realized she was trying to sing. Maybe she had a cold, he thought, although that would be a kind interpretation. She sounded terrible.

But it wasn't until he peered around the forsythia bushes that he realized she stood naked in the grass, less than two yards away.

A pair of fireflies lit sparks of light above her head, then disappeared at the hiss of water. The hose nozzle, hanging from a branch, formed a makeshift shower that sent twinkling drops of water shooting onto her skin.

Suddenly, it all made sense—her secretiveness, her delight that he'd be gone. She wanted a shower, a private one with no surprise visitors interrupting. He had to smile at her cleverness. She'd strung hoses across the yard, filled them with water, then left them to warm in the sunshine. And when the sun went down, she'd taken advantage of the privacy darkness provided. Or should have provided.

He told himself to creep away as quietly as he'd come. But his legs wouldn't obey his common sense. He couldn't drag his eyes from the glistening trails of water streaming down her pale body or the soapy trail of bubbles that escaped her hair, dropping to her shoulders and rolling to the tips of her small, rounded breasts.

She was a water nymph, dancing in the moonlight as she soaped and scrubbed and rinsed. Her movements were hurried, as if she suspected the warm water would cease at any moment. Then, she set the washcloth aside and stretched, clasping her hands above her head and swaying from side to side. She stood that way for what seemed like eternity before springing away with a light shriek. The cold water, he thought, smiling with bemusement.

She didn't bother to dry off, but wrapped herself in a short robe and headed toward the back porch. As she passed the garden shed, she turned off the hydrant, then continued on.

From his position by the bushes, Sam followed her movements through the house as she switched lights on and off. He imagined her pulling down the heavy blue spread in the master bedroom and falling damp and naked to the sheets, cooled by the breeze drifting through the window.

He stood up, shaking himself mentally. She hadn't taken Ben's room at the west corner, but the airy guest room at the east end. He'd seen her silhouette on the curtain before the light blinked out. So why had he imagined her in that big, soft bed?

The question haunted him. She haunted him long after he'd returned home and crawled between the sheets of his own bed.

She belonged to another place and another man. He told himself he'd do well to remember that. But no matter what his mind said, his heart had begun a yearning he'd thought he would never feel again.

He groaned and reached for his discarded jeans. Might as well do something instead of staring at the ceiling and dreaming about what he couldn't have. He could start sorting the junk in that room down the hall.

_____ **FOUR** _____

Hilary glanced around the discreetly lit restaurant in the heart of Chicago's downtown loop, noting the faint clink of good china and the hushed murmurs from other tables. This was Kyle's restaurant of choice for important occasions—their first date, his proposal of marriage, and the celebration of certain high-dollar commissions he'd received. But the expensively contrived atmosphere was wasted on her tonight.

She supposed their first evening together in weeks could be construed as a reason to celebrate. Since she'd returned from Missouri three weeks ago, she'd had no more than a few moments here and there to spare. Until now.

"Kyle, I don't want to talk about this now. Maybe after I get used to the idea of being unemployed. Or better yet, when I start a new job," she insisted, twirling the slender stem of the wine glass between her fingers. A little more pressure, and it would snap, much like her temper was threatening to do.

"You can get another job later, if you want to. Meanwhile, you'll have plenty of time to settle things in Missouri, and, of course, to make wedding plans."

Hilary sighed and rubbed the tight spot at the back of her neck. "Maybe we should wait awhile."

"If that's what you want," he replied. His brows knit in bewildered hurt as he studied her across the table.

She couldn't hold his gaze. Since she'd returned from Missouri, Kyle had pressed hard for a wedding date. Two days ago, a call from Grandpa Bob's attorney had removed her last argument, the uncertain state of her inheritance.

She was free to plan her future, to do as she liked with Grandpa Bob's house, the property in Missouri, and the other assets. She wasn't fantastically wealthy, but she had a nice, comfortable nest egg. Her reluctance to invest that nest egg in hers and Kyle's joint future struck a chord of unease she couldn't explain. She didn't understand it. It was simply there, nibbling away at her confidence, whispering that her relationship with Kyle wasn't all it should be. If it were, Sam Langford's bare chest and mocking grin wouldn't have unsettled her so. And his image wouldn't keep popping into her mind.

"Let's talk about the wedding when I get another job. Or maybe even sooner, in a day or two when I've had a chance to get used to the idea of being unemployed."

"Actually, I'd think you wouldn't be in a hurry to go back to work," Kyle said. "Your inheritance gave you a nice financial cushion that I envy. You can afford to wait until the right job comes along. In the meantime, take a long vacation."

She stared down at the fetuccini she'd twisted around her fork, then untwisted it for lack of something better to do. He was partly right, she knew. But the thought didn't make her feel any better. She was unemployed as of 5 P.M. today. It was a circumstance she'd never experienced, and it didn't sit well.

She'd worked in her parents' restaurant from the time she was old enough to tear lettuce until she'd moved to Grandpa Bob's Chicago home near the university and switched to an office job. The Neill heritage of hard work and thrift was too deeply ingrained for her to take Kyle's suggestion seriously. Even after he could afford to, Grandpa Bob hadn't moved from the simple home he and Grandma had bought when they were newlyweds. He preferred to spend his money on travel, investments, and Hilary's education.

"Maybe I'll take a day or so to catch up on sleep," she said, capitulating only slightly. "But then I'll have to start some serious job hunting."

"You made the right choice," he insisted. "You couldn't have taken the transfer to New York, sweetheart. We wouldn't have had much of a marriage with you gone most of the time."

"I know," she replied, although his reassurance didn't warm her as it should have. Maybe it was depression over losing her job, although she should be grateful she'd at least been offered a choice. Most of the others in her department hadn't. And she had no right to resent the fact that Kyle hadn't even considered relocating to accommodate her career. The fact that she did told her they'd somehow lost the thread of common ambition that had bound them together from the beginning and fed their attraction for one another.

"I have an idea," she began. "Why don't you take a week off. We could go somewhere."

Kyle's eyes widened. "You're kidding?" he asked in an incredulous tone. "Just like that?"

"Why not?"

"Because the last time you involved me in one of your impetuous little adventures, I ended up losing two big commissions. I worked two months on that shopping center deal. Then David Barns slipped in and stole my commission while we camped out in that mausoleum you inherited," he replied in an exasperated tone as he stabbed at a piece of steak.

Hilary gritted her teeth. He'd hit upon a sore point, one she didn't want to discuss at the moment. She didn't think she could without shouting, not in her present frame of mind.

"Forget it," she said. "I should work on my resumé and start checking the ads, anyway."

With a sidelong glance at her mutinous expression, Kyle changed the subject. "Have you looked at that plat for the farm?"

"Gee, do you think it'll rain tomorrow? I hope not," she said, glaring pointedly across the table.

"All right, all right," he said. "I can take a hint."

But he couldn't, she decided later as he parked the car in front of the house. Only a few blocks from Northeastern Illinois University campus, the neighborhood was a curious mixture of students, families, and retirees of all shapes, sizes, and cultures. It was comfortable, but it wasn't Kyle's style. Or maybe she wasn't his style either, she thought peevishly.

"I know you don't want to talk about this tonight," he persisted, as he switched off the engine. "But you have to decide sometime. The sooner the better, really. I'd rather have this behind us before the wedding."

"All right," she capitulated. "I'll look the papers over tomorrow. I'll let you know what I think."

"Good," he said, dropping a kiss on her nose.

She placed a hand on his arm, halting him before he could climb out of the car. "Why don't you go on home?" she said. "I'm pretty tired. I think I'd rather be alone. I probably wouldn't be much company, anyway."

"You're sure?"

"Positive," she said.

"I'd thought maybe I could go over the plat with you, review the projections and all, maybe help you decide a bit quicker."

Hilary's temper exploded. "Damn the plat," she replied. "And damn you for running the subject into the ground. You act as though it's your land, not mine."

"Of course not," he replied, looking wounded. "I'm just trying to help you out. And since I have a bit more expertise in real estate than you—"

"You may know real estate, but you don't seem to know me very well," she replied. "I've had it with your well-intended advice and interference. I'll come to a decision in my own sweet time, and until then I wish you'd keep your mouth shut about it."

"I didn't realize you felt that way. I was only trying to help you look at this from a more businesslike perspective," he argued.

"Meaning?" Her voice was deceptively calm. She waited to see whether he'd cross the line she'd implicitly drawn.

"You're too sentimental for your own good, sweetheart," he explained. "You tend to be impetuous. When you learned you'd inherited your great uncle's farm, you had to fly down there the next day to see it. And look at the mess your impetuosity caused."

The fact that he could call Neill House something as common as a farm delineated the growing differences between them, Hilary fumed to herself. "Kyle, I think I'd better go in before either of us says something regrettable," she said, jerking the door handle and climbing out. "I'll call you tomorrow."

Not waiting for his answer, she hurried to the door and let herself in.

She ground her teeth in silent anger as she kicked

off her shoes and plopped down onto the couch. He'd crossed the line all right. The damned thing was, he was partly right. She did sometimes act impetuously. But not irresponsibly. She wondered if Kyle recognized the difference. It was a sobering thought.

Other incidents crept unbidden to her mind, such as the day she'd surprised him at his office with an impromptu picnic. He'd thanked her for the sandwich, then made phone calls to clients the entire hour she was there. At the time, she'd blamed herself for not checking to see whether he had important business to attend to. Later, she'd wondered whether some of those calls couldn't have waited for a half hour or so.

And then there was the expensive lamb's wool sweater from the shop on Michigan Avenue. She'd bought it because the amorphous banks of blues and grays reminded her of the patchy mist over Lake Michigan the morning she'd met him. She'd guessed the size, only to discover it didn't matter. Kyle didn't like to wear sweaters and had consigned it to the top shelf of the closet. Yet she'd worn his ostentatious rock of an engagement ring without a murmur of protest, even though it seemed garish compared with the modest solitaire she would have picked if given a choice.

She used to think they balanced one another, her eye for detail and his ability to grasp the overall picture and choose the most advantageous path. She'd thought them well matched, with the same upward goals and business sense. Now she wasn't so sure.

If only he had a little more of her sense of fun and maybe a little of Sam Langford's sentimentality. Come to think of it, if she could just throw the two men into the blender, she might come up with the perfect mix.

Hilary grimaced. Maybe her foul mood had colored her sense of perspective. She'd worked long hours these past weeks, yet the end didn't bring the sense of relief she'd imagined. Just a sense of exhaustion that reminded her of how much sleep she'd missed lately.

That was what she needed, she told herself as she rose from the couch and shuffled into the bedroom. Precious hours of sleep, with no chirping alarm clock to wake her before the sun rose. She could sleep as long as she wanted tomorrow and then go for a long walk in Lincoln Park. And sometime in the next few days, she'd unpack the boxes she'd brought home from the office.

But sleep evaded her until the small hours. After her conscious mind finally succumbed, her dreams were filled with the same swirling questions that had kept her awake. She awoke the next morning feeling unrested and vaguely uneasy about those dreams. Disjointed images of Sam Langford sprang to mind, but Kyle had been only a shadowy figure.

The old adage was wrong. Nothing looked clearer in the morning. Her life had become too complicated for simple answers.

Hilary sighed loudly, then grinned at the melodramatic sound. Rolling over, she dialed her mother's number at work. She needed a good dose of Marianne Neill's common sense.

"Yes?" Her mother's brief greeting indicated the restaurant hadn't opened for business yet. Even so, she could hear pots banging in the background and, closer, the sound of something sizzling on the grill.

"Hi, Mom. Do you have a minute, or should I call back later?"

"Oh, honey, hold on just a minute." Her voice faded away, and Hilary could picture her mother, tucking the receiver against her ample middle, while she shouted something at the cook. "Let me call you right back on the office phone," she said a moment later.

Hilary replaced the receiver and piled her pillows

into a comfortable bedrest while she waited. Maybe she'd visit Mom and Dad for a week or so. A few days at the small German restaurant in the little downstate town might restore her sense of perspective. Mom's sauerbraten alone would be worth the trip, not to mention the beirochs.

Governed more by her stomach than her mind, she snatched up the phone halfway through the first ring. "What's today's special?" she asked, wondering if the sizzle she'd heard was the meat for the beirochs.

"I have a house in Oak Brook that looks good. You'll have to move quickly, though. I already have a contingency offer," Kyle replied. His voice in her ear jarred her out of her pleasant daydreams.

"Sorry, I thought it was Mom," she replied. "She's supposed to call me right back."

"Then I won't keep you. I called to apologize for upsetting you last night," he said. "I should have realized you'd be depressed about leaving your job."

Hilary hesitated, choosing her words carefully before she spoke. "It wasn't just the job."

"You're still angry about the plat?" His tone cooled perceptibly, giving her the impression he was about to lose his temper. But Kyle didn't erupt in a burst of anger. He froze you out.

"No," she replied, rolling her eyes toward the ceiling. She was, but saying so would only worsen the situation.

"I'm tired, and not just physically. The last few months have been unsettling, to say the least. I think I need time to think. I have a lot of decisions to make, and I don't feel like making them yet."

That said, she tensed as the silence stretched between them.

"Okay," Kyle finally answered. "I suppose I can

understand that. Maybe we can talk about things at dinner tonight.''

"I don't think so.''

"Why not?''

Her spirits sank at the frost in his voice. He didn't understand at all. "I'm driving down to Mom's this afternoon. I'm not sure how long I'll be gone,'' she said. "I'll call you in a few days.''

As soon as she heard the dial tone, she punched in the restaurant's phone number.

"Your line was busy,'' Marianne Neill accused after ascertaining it was her daughter.

"Kyle called,'' she said.

"How is he?'' Her tone was noncommittal, but Marianne Neill had reservations about Kyle's suitability as a son-in-law. She'd voiced them once, then left Hilary to decide on her own.

"He's exasperating. He's just so damn pushy. I know he has to be in his job. I just never expected him to be that way with me. I'm starting to think you might have been right about him.''

"Come for a visit,'' her mother suggested. "It'll give you both a little time to cool off and think things through. Or maybe you'd rather go over to Neill House and spend some time on your own. You might learn something about your father's side of the family.''

"No, Mom. I'd much rather spend time with you and Dad,'' Hilary protested, then hesitated. Maybe her mother had stumbled upon a solution. "Though maybe I should go over there for a week or two and clear up some loose ends. I could use a vacation, anyway, and maybe I'll figure out why Grandpa Bob talked so much about the place.'' *Maybe a couple of conversations with Sam Langford would irritate her enough to chase him out of her dreams.*

"You'll stop and spend the night with us at least?''

"Of course, Mom. I'll be there before you close tonight. Save me some sauerbraten."

Despite having driven for seven hours that day, Hilary felt more relaxed than she had in weeks. As she rounded the last curve before Sam's and Uncle Ben's mailboxes, she decided this trip was one of her better ideas. Maybe it was the comfort of Mom's cooking or the cheerful, unjudgmental way her family had listened to her problems. They didn't pry for details she didn't want to divulge or fill her ears with advice. They wouldn't until she asked.

Perhaps, too, her worries were eased by the calming influence of the open spaces she'd driven through for the last two days.

She'd felt the first uncoiling of the tension in her shoulders a few miles out of the suburbs. By the time she reached Bloomington, she'd dusted off some of her old tapes and was singing along with Mick Jagger.

Today, she'd put Mick aside and flipped from station to station as she crossed Missouri. The drive took longer than she'd anticipated, thanks to the constant rain that poured from gray skies until she was within twenty miles of her destination. But the slower pace gave her time to think and formulate a plan of action.

First, she'd take a good look around Neill House and evaluate Kyle's ideas. Then she'd see what other options were open to her. That way, no matter what she eventually decided, she'd be sure she hadn't overlooked something important. She ought to consider the rest of her life in those terms as well—her career and her relationship with Kyle. Too many times, she'd followed his lead rather than risk hurting his feelings or making him angry. Maybe if she'd forced a compromise sooner, he wouldn't have been so startled when she'd objected to his handling of Neill House.

Putting the thought aside for the moment, she turned into Sam's drive. He waved, then bent over and rummaged under the truck seat. *Nice rear, even better than Kyle's.* Her mouth dried as he leaned further inside and stretched, tightening the fabic over his buttocks and down his thighs. *Look away, you idiot.* But her eyes refused to obey until he retrieved a can, tossed it into a sack, and turned around.

She concentrated on unbuckling her seat belt, and by the time she had her blush under control, he was reaching back into the truck. Weighted down with two stacks of groceries, he returned her greeting with a nod and kicked the pickup door shut. In his tweed jacket, tie, and pleated corduroys, he looked more like the teacher he claimed to be. Except she couldn't remember having a college professor who looked remotely that good. Maybe the history department attracted more interesting types than the business college.

"Did you just get in or have you been out running errands?" he asked when she climbed out of the car and stretched self-consciously.

"Just got here," she answered. "Did you get my message?" He didn't just look good. He sounded good, even pleased to see her. She needed that now, a little reassurance that she was worth knowing. Kyle's chilly good-bye had cut a hole in her self-confidence.

"Sure did," he said with a warm smile. "You barely missed the plumber."

"Took his good old time fixing that, didn't he?"

Sam shrugged. "Nobody lives there. Kind of makes it low priority, wouldn't you say? He said he's finished up there. He had to replace the entire water line between the pump shed and the house. It must have been fifty years old. He'll send the bill to the attorney."

"Good. I don't think I want to know the amount

for awhile yet," she said. "Can I help you with th. groceries?"

"You could get the door. The keys are in my pocket."

Hilary gaped. Was he serious? Looking was one thing, but she wasn't interested in a game of slap and tickle. It had never been her style, and it was even more out of the question now.

"My jacket pocket," he specified.

She felt herself flush. "That's what I thought," she lied. She reached into his pocket and retrieved the small ring of keys, taking great care not to touch him anywhere else.

"Got'em," she said, tossing them high and catching them. "Which one opens the front door?"

"The round one."

The key worked easily in the lock and the door swung open, letting a blast of cold air escape.

"You have air conditioning?" she said, stepping into the central hall and rubbing her arms. The rain had cooled the air outdoors to an unseasonable low for this time of year, according to the last weather report she'd heard. Inside, however, it was positively freezing.

"Forgot to turn it off this morning. Could you hit the switch for me?" he asked, indicating a window unit at the end of the hall.

"Of course," she replied, hurrying over. She punched a button, then followed him into the kitchen and helped him stow the perishables. That finished, she saw no further excuse to linger, except for the fact that he was blocking the only route out of the kitchen.

"By the way," he began, "I've been going through some boxes, and there's a family piece you should have, a pearl necklace, that was Sarah's."

Hilary hesitated. "The one from the portrait?"

He nodded. "I didn't realize you'd seen it. The necklace has been in the family for generations. It's yours by right.''

Hilary shook her head. "You keep it. If Sarah or Ben had intended anything else, there would have been some mention of it in the will or the other papers the attorney had.'' She smiled, changing the subject. "I'd better get up to the house and put my own stuff away,'' she said, waiting for him to step out of the narrow aisle between the cabinets and the table. He didn't move.

"There's no rush. I picked up an extra steak in case you stopped by. I didn't know whether you'd take the time to pick up groceries.'' His voice unnerved her, despite his casual tone. It wasn't a frightening feeling, but a budding warmth that teased a reluctant smile to her lips. He seemed more like a welcoming friend than the wary neighbor he'd been until now. It was a step in the right direction, although she'd better move slowly or he might misinterpret her motives.

She shook her head. "I have a whole ice chest full of frozen meals, courtesy of my mother.''

He raised his brows thoughtfully as he shrugged out of the jacket and slung it over the chair back. "You brought food from Chicago? Somehow I didn't think you were the type to plan ahead that much.''

"I'm not. Mom's place is along the way. I stayed with her last night. She froze up extras from the restaurant yesterday.''

"I see,'' he said. But in spite of his smile, she sensed he was disappointed.

"Maybe tomorrow you could have some of Mom's sauerbraten with me,'' she found herself asking before she thought.

His smile turned warm. "Sauerbraten you said? What time?''

"What's good for you?''

"Sauerbraten,'' he mused. "Somehow, the steak is

losing its appeal. How about we hit your cooler tonight?''

Hilary couldn't help but laugh at the little-boy anticipation shining in his dark eyes. He seemed younger than she'd remembered, or maybe she'd imagined the underlying sadness in his expression last time she was here. God knows, he'd had reason to be melancholy, losing his wife as he had. Perhaps she'd let her knowledge of his loss overshadow her perception of him.

''Sounds like a plan,'' she replied.

''Good. Give me a few minutes to change, then I'll ride up with you.'' He was already loosening his tie and unbuttoning his shirt collar.

The room suddenly seemed too warm. ''Come over whenever you're ready. I think I'll go on ahead and get things started.''

To her relief he agreed. ''That might work better anyway. I need to make a couple of quick calls.''

He backed out into the living room, stepping aside so she could pass as he unbuttoned his cuffs.

''I'll walk up in a few minutes,'' he said.

''See you then,'' she replied, hurrying out. She practically ran to the car and flung herself inside. The car purred to life with a quick turn of the key. She was out of the drive and halfway to Uncle Ben's house before she even focused on what she was doing.

What was she doing? Kyle would have a fit if he knew she was dining alone with her nutty caretaker, as he referred to Sam. But Kyle didn't even know she was in Missouri. He thought she was at her mother's place.

Although Hilary felt guilty about deceiving him, she wasn't ready to call him yet. She didn't want to argue anymore. And that, too, was reason enough not to mention this little dinner when she did eventually talk to him.

Both gates were open so she reached the house in a

matter of minutes. The banks of daylilies bordering the last stretch of the drive were in full bloom, welcoming her with hundreds of trumpet-shaped blossoms waving in the wind. The rambler roses along the fence still sported a few late flowers, but only the bright-pink rose hips were left of the main flush of bloom. They must have been breathtaking a month ago.

She wished she had time now to walk around to see what changes the summer had brought, and take a closer look at those white flowers down by the pond. Later, she promised herself.

As soon as she'd parked, she grabbed her suitcases and carried them up to the bedroom she'd used before. Then she hurried out to the car for the cooler. She'd just opened the back door when she caught a faint whiff of something unpleasant. She thought at first it smelled like gas, the odd artificial scent of propane or piped natural gas. Then it was gone. She sniffed again, but caught only the musky scent of damp earth mingled with the faint, oily smell of her car engine. It wasn't gas. She must have imagined it or mistaken the scent.

Back inside, it took only a moment to put the food into the oven to heat. Then she put a pan of water on the front burner under a high flame. While she waited for it to boil, she set the table.

When she returned to the stove to check the water, it was barely warm. The flame had blown out, leaving a hint of gas smell in the air. After turning off the burner to let the lingering gas fumes clear, she closed the door to the screened-in porch. After a moment, she tried to turn the burner back on. It wouldn't work. A quick check showed the oven was off, too.

"Damned antique," she muttered, lifting the drip pans. "Wouldn't you know it." The pilot light was out as well. If she was going to spend much time here, a new stove was in order. But she wasn't, she reminded herself, so she'd just have to make do with this relic. Uncle Benjamin had probably installed it at the same time as the old water line. The old man hadn't taken the renovations far enough in her opinion.

She struck a match to relight the pilot.

"Hilary!" Sam called from the porch. "Get outside now."

"Just a minute," she shouted, fiddling with the stove. The pilot light wouldn't catch. She flipped the burner off and sniffed. She couldn't even smell gas. Maybe the line was clogged somehow.

"Hilary, damn it!" The kitchen door flew open and slammed hard against the wall.

She stood speechless, staring at the crazed man Sam had become. She actually took a step backward when he practically leaped in her direction, then grabbed her wrist and dragged her outside.

"Stop this," she retorted, genuinely afraid of him now. "What's wrong with you?"

"I think you have a propane leak. I smelled it when I came around the corner of the house," he replied, sagging against the sturdy trunk of a large oak. "Sorry I scared you. But when you didn't come out after I called you—" His voice trailed off, vibrating with a hint of panic.

Hilary started to speak, then stopped, remembering the smell she'd dismissed earlier. "I thought, well never mind. Do you know how to turn the gas off?"

"That's the first thing I did," he said, and her eyes strayed involuntarily to the bulbous propane tank at the side of the house. That explained her trouble with the stove. No fuel, thus no flame.

"Then there's not much of a problem now. I'll get the food, and we can eat at your house. In a couple of hours any leftover gas should be cleared out," she said, already walking away.

"No! You're not going in there," he shouted, grabbing her and pulling her back.

"Sam, you're overreacting. I can't smell anything now."

"Not a chance," he said, starting down the drive. Since he held her hand in a firm grip, she had little choice but to go, too, or be dragged in the gravel.

"What about the sauerbraten?"

"Damn the sauerbraten. I'll take you to the Berliner Bear for dinner," he said.

"And after that?" she challenged.

"You can sleep at my house. We'll get somebody out here tomorrow to fix the leak."

"That does it," she retorted. He'd gone too far. She was heartily sick of take-charge men who acted as if she couldn't make a basic decision concerning her own well-being. She planted her feet, suddenly halting. His momentum nearly jerked her along anyway, but she held her ground.

"No," she said, when he turned around and retraced his steps.

"No, what?"

"No, I'm not going out to dinner with you. No, I'm not sleeping at your house. And no, *we* are not going to get somebody out here to fix the leak tomorrow. You can damn well butt out of my business," she answered, ending on a shout.

"Yeah?"

"Yeah," she retorted, then wavered at the determined look in his tawny brown eyes. Before she could think to run, he leaped forward and scooped her up, pitching her over his shoulder.

She kicked hard, but he caught her legs behind the knees in one firm grip and balanced her with the other hand on her rear end. He carried her that way, kicking and screaming, until she began to get dizzy from all the blood rushing to her head.

By the time they reached the first gate, she'd quieted a bit. Another twenty paces down the drive she was in agony. She let her body go limp until she felt him relax his hold a bit. Still, she stifled the impulse to wriggle free. She'd probably tumble them both to the rocks. After rounding the bend in the drive, he stopped and carefully set her on her feet.

Hilary pinched her eyes shut, waiting for the ground to steady beneath her.

"Are you all right?" Sam said, still holding her around the waist.

She nodded, then stepped back and slugged him in the breadbasket. Unfortunately, it hurt her more than it hurt him. Either that, or he was one hell of a faker, despite the faint grunt he emitted when her fist made contact.

"Damn you," she muttered. "What do you have there, a steel plate?"

"I wish," he replied, gingerly touching his stomach. So, she'd hurt him after all, she thought with satisfaction.

"You deserved it, you know," she said. "I don't like cave-man tactics."

"I'll do it again if you try to go back to the house," he replied.

She believed him. He looked ready to spring at her slightest movement in that direction.

"Don't you think you're overreacting a bit?" she suggested.

"I have to be sure it's safe. Propane is tricky. It pools in low places like basements. It's not something you fool around with," he replied. "I ought to know. I lost my wife because of her father's leaky furnace valve."

Hilary gasped. "I'm sorry," she replied. "I'd forgotten."

"I know you think I overreacted, and maybe I did," he replied, pulling her closer. "But it's just not worth the chance."

She stared up, transfixed by the emotions revealed in his face. He pulled her closer, too close for her eyes to focus. His lips touched hers, gently and tenderly, communicating the depth of his fear. It touched her more deeply than any declaration of passion, any promise of love ever had. It made her forget they were barely friends. It made her forget they stood in full view of the county road. Worst of all, it made her forget Kyle.

FIVE

The sweet intensity captured her, touched her to the soul with butterfly caresses. Molten heat passed through her, fed by the trembling of his fingers against her skin.

His hands cupped her face, holding her like fragile hand-blown glass while his lips moved against hers, with hers. It felt right.

But it wasn't. It couldn't be. She was kissing the wrong man.

He must have felt her hesitation because his hands tightened on her arms, even as he lifted his head. She drew a shaky breath as her glance slid away. *What just happened?*

"Hilary?"

She told herself not to look at him, but the quaver of uncertainty in his voice reached past her few remaining defenses. He watched her, probably seeing too much. She was too shaken to hide the emotions still rampaging through her, confusion, anger, and most especially this unwanted desire. She was simply too vulnerable right now, too needy. She tried to pull her face into a mask and knew by his expression she hadn't succeeded. Her insides quivered as the lines around his eyes softened, then crinkled into a smile.

"You're not going to punch me again, are you?"

She grimaced. "I'm thinking about it. You shouldn't have kissed me. I shouldn't have allowed it to happen," she replied, gaining control over her voice as she pulled away. He let her go.

"I know," he said. "I'm miles ahead of you."

Hilary was so upset about her own reactions to the kiss, to his nearness, that it took a moment for his words to register.

"What are you talking about?"

"You kissed me back."

She stared at the daylilies waving their trumpet heads a few feet from where they stood. "I didn't."

"My mistake," he replied.

The smile in his voice made her blush with shame. She had responded to his kiss, and the knowledge disturbed her.

"You surprised me, that's all. It was just reaction, and, well, I don't know what. It doesn't mean anything."

"Doesn't it?"

She shook her head vehemently. "It was just circumstances," she insisted, spinning on her heel. She took off down the driveway at a fast clip, not waiting to see if he followed. She wanted to run away, but what remained of her dignity wouldn't permit flight. Besides, that would give the entire incident credence, make it important. And it wasn't. It was just an aberration born of the moment and never to be repeated. She was engaged to Kyle. Even if her engagement rested on a rocky foundation lately, she was still committed to him. And until she returned the ring, she had no right to feel anything, to share anything with another man.

"It was more than circumstances," Sam called after her.

"You're wrong," she shouted.

"Believe what you want, for now."

She halted. "That's the trouble with you, Sam," she began as he closed the distance between them with several loping strides. "You're so caught up in your soldier games, and your history books, and maybe even your memories, that you don't recognize reality when it hits you in the face."

He rested a hand on his stomach and shot her a pained, pointed look. "Oh?"

"Oh, my foot," she retorted. "Think about it. You smell gas. You panic, justifiably considering what happened to your wife and her parents. And for a minute, just a minute, mind you, it's *déjà vu*. It wasn't me that you were kissing, not really. It had nothing to do with me."

Some strong emotion registered for an instant in the depths of his eyes, then he blinked it away. He shrugged, pulling nonchalance around him like a child hiding in a favorite blanket.

"I knew who I was kissing. Did you?"

A hot pang struck her midsection and radiated in trembling waves to her outer limbs. Before she could think of an appropriate denial, he turned and headed toward Ben's house, her house now.

Puzzlement gradually overtook the sensual confusion that held her speechless. Why was he returning to the place he'd just fled like a cat from a pack of street dogs? He stepped off the gravel drive and unlatched the wide gate that weeks before had kept cattle from wandering into the yard to trample the daylilies and tear at the roses. He swung it from its position against the fence, closing off entrance to Neill House.

Hilary turned away, not wanting to watch anymore.

He confused her, yet drew her in a way she couldn't explain. Maybe it was the attraction of opposites, a weird fascination with the differences. Or maybe she was just susceptible to the charm of this place and the man who fit in as if it was his heritage instead of hers. Coming on the heels of her disagreements with Kyle, the kiss ignited fantasies she had barely acknowledged, fantasies of being cherished and protected.

Real life wasn't that way—at least not her life. And she wouldn't want it to be. She was no kitchen mouse. She was her own woman. She needed a partner, not a protector. Kyle might be a difficult partner, but she had a lot more in common with him than with a tweedy professor who played cowboys and Indians on weekends.

Lost in her thoughts, she reached the county road without realizing she'd even been walking. Glancing back, she saw that Sam had nearly caught up with her. His guarded expression touched a spot of guilt. He might be a nut, but he'd acted with the best of intentions and may have actually saved her from harm. She'd been waving a lit match around and cursing the stove when she should have been investigating that peculiar smell.

The kiss? Well, it was simply a reaction to the situation. It was only a big deal if she made it one. So, she forced her thoughts elsewhere.

Leaning against the squat, stone gatepost at the end of the drive, she stared out across the field. Already, the grass had turned brown from the heat and lack of rain. Evidently, the deluge she'd driven through on the highway hadn't left more than a smattering in the dust here. It reminded her of the summer when one of the two city wells in her hometown had run dry and they'd had to ration water. She frowned. She ought to be thinking of practical details like that instead of fighting with the caretaker. Or explaining away kisses.

"Do I have a well?" she asked as Sam swung the second wide stock gate closed.

"Beg your pardon?" he asked, throwing her a puzzled look.

"A well," she repeated. "I never thought to ask whether the house was on a rural water system."

"That's why you waited for me?"

"What were you expecting?"

"I'm not sure, an apology for that jab in the stomach. Or maybe even a mildly armed truce." Amusement twinkled in his eyes. "Certainly not a discussion on infrastructure."

Hilary crossed her arms. "You deserved that punch. I do appreciate the fact that you noticed the gas leak, though." It was as close as she'd get to an apology. She certainly wasn't sorry for the things she'd said. They were true, weren't they? As for the kiss, she'd pretend it never happened and maybe he'd take the hint.

Sam nodded in comprehension, giving her the impression that she'd once again let her thoughts show too plainly on her face. He leaned against the gate to nudge the latch into place.

"Since you're at least speaking to me, I can assume you've forgiven me. I can trust you not to attack me with a steak knife when my back is turned."

"As long as you don't turn into a Neanderthal again."

He winked, then started across the road. "Can't promise what I can't guarantee. You know how we cave men are, all impulses and no brains to back them up."

Relieved that he'd decided not to push the issue, she caught up with him. "Right. Now, tell me about the water. Do I have a well or a water bill?"

"Both. The water around here doesn't taste too good, so Ben tied into the water district line when it came through. The deep well's still operational, though. He used it for the livestock and his gardens."

"So that's why the outdoor hydrants worked when the water line was broken."

"That's right. Guess I didn't think to explain that at the time. I was thinking of—" His eyes met hers in the brief hesitation. "Other things," he finished.

Hilary knew what "other things" he meant, and she willed herself not to blush. "It doesn't matter. I was just curious," she said.

"Idle curiosity or is there a purpose behind the question?" he asked as they crossed the lawn toward his front porch.

"In other words, does the water supply situation affect any plans I might have for the property?" she surmised, then continued without waiting for his answer. "Probably, but I'll leave those details to Kyle once I decide on the general plan. Real estate is his specialty, not mine." Something flared in Sam's eyes at the mention of Kyle's name.

Sam hesitated on the bottom step, turning to face her. "You're the number cruncher. I'd think costs would be your territory."

She grimaced inwardly. She hated all those little nicknames people who spent money used for those who kept track of it. "I'd rather not argue with you now. Can't we talk about something else? Something benign, such as the weather or the going price for corn futures?"

"Or the price of toilet paper in China?"

"Or the lack of good study habits among today's youth," she added with a teasing smile.

He crossed the porch and held the screen door open. "Now, that's an invitation to an earful," he warned her. "You would not believe some of the weird excuses these kids come up with. Or some of the convoluted, unsupported arguments they call research papers."

Hilary barely contained a sigh of relief as she followed him inside. He'd followed her lead into safer territory. "I'll bet you go through a lot of red ink."

"And a lot of aspirin," he admitted.

"And I thought only accountants got headaches," she teased.

"Your numbers don't back talk, do they?"

"The day they do, I'm checking into the nearest mental hospital," she replied. "Where's your phone? I need to call the propane company—R&R Bottle Gas, isn't it? Or do you suppose the plumber bumped the gas lines when he was fixing the water line?"

"It's possible," he agreed. He pointed to an alcove under the stairs where an older, rotary dial desktop phone rested atop a 1950s-era telephone table and chair combo. "The book's in the cabinet underneath. Randy Swale is the plumber. You'll probably have to catch him at home or leave a message with his wife."

Hilary nodded and reached for the phone book, pretending to concentrate on the listings until the creaking floors signaled his presence in the kitchen. She'd half expected him to insist on making the calls, but he didn't show so much as a raised eyebrow when she took charge of the task. His high-handedness must be limited to panic situations.

The propane company was closed, so she left a message on its recorder. It took a little longer to track down the plumber, but eventually she located him at the third number his wife suggested. He offered to come over immediately. However, the weariness in his voice prompted Hilary to insist the next morning would be soon enough. With the gas shut off, there was little danger, even though she couldn't convince Sam of that fact.

"All taken care of?" Sam asked when she stepped into the living room a moment later. He glanced up from his desk where he was sorting a stack of papers.

"Until tomorrow. So, what's for dinner?"

"Steak if we stay here, or we could go out some-place—the Berliner Bear, if your taste buds are set for German food."

Hilary hesitated and shook her head. Being alone with him like this made her edgy. Facing him over a restaurant table could prove more than awkward. Better to keep it casual, a friendly snack between neighbors who were just getting acquainted. "Steak sounds fine. And quick. I'm starving."

"Me, too," he admitted. "Although I'm really sorry about the food we left, but don't even suggest going back to put it away," he added before she could speak.

"Not in this lifetime," she muttered. She didn't think her nerves would survive another forcible demon-stration of strength—or a repeat of what had happened afterward. "How do you like your steak?"

"I'm supposed to ask you," he said, leading the way into the kitchen. He retrieved a cola from the refrigera-tor and offered her one.

She studied him as he took a long sip. The light from the window behind him threw his face into shadow, giving his half-closed eyes a hooded, mysterious look. His lean, muscled arms flexed with the movement, then relaxed as he lowered the can. For an instant, she let herself remember the feel of his lips on hers, then she pushed the thought away. She ought to turn her back on him and run, but she wasn't that much of a coward. Besides, she wanted him on her side in whatever she did with Neill House.

A second later, his eyes met hers. His smile swiftly changed to uneasiness as he caught her studied look.

"What?" he asked. "Is there a bug in my hair?"

She shook her head. "I was only trying to imagine you in the classroom with twenty students hanging onto your every word," she lied.

"Twenty? I should be so lucky. I have three lecture halls of freshmen—about five hundred total. I can't even begin to remember their names."

"Sounds awful. Why do you do it?"

"Because I need to make a living. Isn't that why you became an accountant?"

She grinned back at him. "I guess we all have to do something. I crunch numbers. You crunch knowledge into unwilling minds. Although I would imagine there are a number of other jobs you could do as well."

He rummaged under the sink and pulled out a can of lighter fluid. "You're right. And tonight, I build fires." He released a maniacal laugh worthy of a slasher film and headed for the back door. "You can wait here in the air conditioning, unless you don't mind checking the garden for ripe tomatoes."

Hilary plunked her can down and followed him out. "If I stayed in there, you'd accuse me of being a lazy wimp."

"No, I'd say you preferred to play lady of the manor," he said, softening the jibe with a teasing grin.

"And I'd say you don't know me very well," she said, then immediately regretted her words as she considered the obvious comeback. "Never mind. I'll get the tomatoes."

The kitchen garden wasn't difficult to find. Tucked behind the small barn at the rear of the house, it was fenced around all four sides. The deer tracks in the well-watered soil proved the fence to be less than successful, though.

She was less interested in the ravages of wildlife than the garden itself. It wasn't laid out in neat, straight rows as she'd expected, but in riotous patches of growth with wide, mown patches between the growing beds. A square border of flowers, climbing vegetables, and herbs surrounded the rest, butting up against and rambling over the fence.

Sam's garden was . . . unexpected, like the man himself.

Not wanting to dwell on that thought, she headed toward the staked tomato plants at the far end and started gathering the sun-ripened fruit. Thirty seconds later, she wished she'd brought something to carry them in. A quick glance around proved that Sam was, unfortunately, conscientious about putting tools and buckets away. Hating to admit she'd walked out unprepared, she made a makeshift sling with the bottom of her T-shirt and piled in an armful of red, yellow, and pink tomatoes. She'd meant to pick only a few—until she'd popped one of the sun-warm cherry tomatoes into her mouth and sucked at the tangy juice.

Wandering down the rows, she added a few of the short, finger-thick carrots, cucumbers, baby zucchini, and banana peppers. From the next garden bed, she added a few sprigs of kale and some other green, leafy stuff whose name escaped her.

The heavy load at the bottom of the shirt pulled at the neckline, stretching it out. It probably would never spring back into shape. The shirt sling was awkward, but it worked. And the faint breeze blowing in from the pasture cooled her bared midriff.

Somehow, she managed to maneuver her way out the gate and kick it closed without losing a single vegetable. It wasn't until she reached the porch steps that her load started to slip. She gathered up the edge again, then realized she couldn't manage the doorknob without spilling two fat tomatoes balanced at the top.

"Sam?" she called.

No answer.

She kicked the door with the toe of her shoe, hoping he'd hear the knocking sound. Still no answer.

Her toe was poised to knock a second time when he appeared around the corner, walking slowly.

"Need help?" His glance dropped to the tomatoes, then shifted slightly. The coolness of her midriff intensified and spread, raising the hair on her arms and sending tiny shivers up her spine. Hilary turned away and pretended to adjust her load.

"You could open the door for me," she suggested in what she hoped was a calm, faintly sarcastic tone. She backed away from the door to give him plenty of room.

He managed to touch her anyway, brushing lightly against her shoulder as he passed. She tried to ignore the sensation.

"You didn't have to pick the patch clean," he remarked as he twisted the knob and held the door wide to keep it from swinging back at her. "I do eventually get around to taking care of it." He plucked the slipping tomatoes from the top of her makeshift carrier, this time taking studious care not to bump her. His glance lingered below her chin, in the vicinity of her exposed flesh showing through the gaping neckline.

"I overdid it a bit, didn't I?" she said, talking too fast. "They say you shouldn't go to the grocery store when you're hungry. I guess the same is true of the garden."

"Take home whatever we don't use tonight. It beats anything you'll find in the grocery store."

"Fresh always does," she hesitated when she reached the sink, staring down at the sling. He stepped closer to help before she could decide whether to ask him or risk dropping something when she tried on her own.

She held her breath as he unloaded the vegetables, piling them carefully on the sideboard. He didn't touch her the entire time, and she finally inhaled and turned toward the sink as she retrieved the last carrots and cucumbers herself. Leaning against the sturdy counter would help steady her wobbly knees, but he'd probably notice that, too. She kept her spine straight.

"Did you have something specific in mind when you picked all this, or were you just in the mood to harvest?" he asked.

Hilary glanced over her shoulder, arching her brows slightly as she tried to gauge his thoughts. His expression was undecipherable. "Why don't you wait and see?" she suggested.

He leaned closer still. "Maybe we could work together."

"Maybe you could do the steaks. I like mine medium rare."

He hesitated, smiling distractedly. He reached out, as if to touch her, then his hand dropped to his side. "You have a tomato smear on your chin."

She grabbed a towel and dabbed at her chin. "Did I get it?" she asked, turning for inspection.

Again, his eyes held an uncertain, distracted look. "I think so," he finally answered, his gaze lingering at the spot, then lifting to meet hers. There it was again, that tingling feeling that made her senses sing.

"Well, we'd better get to work or we'll starve to death," she said, trying to the break the spell. She picked up a cherry tomato and tossed it to him, forcing him to catch it or be splattered.

He caught it in midair and popped it into his mouth slowly, deliberately. Hilary spun away and opened the refrigerator. Staring blindly at the contents, she thought she'd never seen a more sensual gesture than Sam's lips slowly closing around that tiny red orb.

"I'll go check the fire," he said, his footsteps already creaking lightly across the worn, hardwood floor. The screen door squeaked, then clicked shut.

Hilary wasn't so gentle with the refrigerator. She heard a clinking inside as she slammed the door, but didn't bother to see what had been knocked over. She was too rattled. The man was dangerous, pure poison to her peace of mind. She'd be damned if she'd let him know it, though.

Returning to the sink, she reached for the faucet, then changed her mind and leaned on tiptoe to peer outside. She stood there a moment, staring out the window until he stepped into sight. He glanced down at the grill, gave a satisfied nod, and looked directly at the kitchen window. Afraid that his sharp brown eyes had caught her peeking between the break in the curtains, she backed away, one hand resting absently at her throat. Her pulse thudded beneath her fingertips, beating so loudly she could hear its rhythmic patter.

Remember Kyle.

She turned on the faucet and listened to the pipes hiss and knock. Clear water streamed into the chipped porcelain basin. She smiled shakily. At least it was clear. After all the commotion from the pipes, she'd half-expected to see flecks of rust or worse. That happened in old houses, as Kyle frequently reminded her. They were going to buy a new one, or a fairly new one at least. Kyle didn't want to deal with problems any previous owners had moved away from.

Kyle. He didn't make her heart pound in her ears anymore. Come to think of it, she couldn't remember his ever affecting her that way. Theirs had been an attraction of the minds, a recognition of equal drive and ambition. And Kyle had proved to be an energetic, inventive lover. Lately, with all the stress of losing her grandfather and then her job, she had needed more. Yet, she didn't know how to ask him because she didn't know exactly what was missing. Maybe that's why she kept having all those crazy thoughts about Sam. She was just feeling unsettled and insecure, and looking for a cure for a problem she couldn't name.

She rinsed her hands, then splashed water on her face, letting the coolness wash away her idiotic thoughts. She'd come to Missouri to get her bearings, not jumble her brain any further. A few quiet days of rest would give her a more reasonable perspective on the situation. She'd probably laugh at ever having felt attracted to someone so very different from herself.

Hilary glanced through the curtains again. Sam was rummaging around in the garden now, though she couldn't imagine why. The rows were free of weeds, and she'd picked enough to last the two of them several days. She couldn't think what she might have missed.

With a wry grin, she turned her attention to washing the vegetables and positioning them on the drainboard so they wouldn't roll off. She was just finishing the carrots when Sam returned. The pungent odor of onions reached the sink before he did.

"Where were the onions?" she asked. She stepped aside so he could rinse the bulbs under the running water. His arm brushed against hers anyway. She tried to ignore the sensation.

"Mixed in with the potatoes. Folklore has it that the onion smell keeps the potato beetles away."

"Does it work?"

He shrugged. "I haven't noticed too many, but there could be other reasons why the bugs aren't so plentiful this year."

"Such as the insecticide you spray," she retorted, hoping to beat him to the punch.

"Possibly. I can't imagine anything wanting to lick up too much of that tobacco juice."

She nearly dropped the carrot. "You spray tobacco juice on the garden?" She wanted to run to the bathroom to rinse out her mouth.

"Of course." He ripped the outer leaves from the onion top and picked at the thin skin of the bulb with his blunt-nailed fingertips. "We found several references to it in nineteenth century farming journals and books. Several of us decided to try some of these old methods to see how well they work. It's not exactly scientific research since we don't have a control garden for comparison."

"I thought that's why they invented insecticides, to kill the bugs better," Hilary answered, then reached for the onion. "Here, give me that. You're mangling it."

"Sometimes the old ways are better. They're certainly safer."

"Oh?" This man was about as different from Kyle as night from day.

He leaned closer. "Take Ben's house, or this one for that matter. Both are well over a century old, yet they're still standing as solid as ever.

"They don't build houses like that anymore," she finished, mimicking her grandfather's tone. She dropped the growl and continued in her normal voice. "I agree. Most of the houses Kyle sells won't be standing in fifty years, let alone a hundred and fifty. But that's not the point."

"All right. What is?"

"Neither of the two houses in question is in its original condition. You and Ben, and other people before you, took the best of the past and added central heating, modern plumbing—or what passed for modern fifty years ago. Now, you have most of the comforts and conveniences the present technology has to offer. The same is true of just about anything else, fertilizer included.''

''Newer is better,'' he suggested. The challenge that glittered in his eyes seemed to radiate through him, tensing him like a cat ready to spring. It affected her as well, raising her guard, yet fine-tuning all her senses. She lifted her chin and mentally honed her argument.

''Sometimes,'' she replied, dragging the word out as she turned away from him. ''Where do you keep the knives?''

They were still arguing an hour later when the steaks were nothing but cleaned bones on dirty plates. The cut, herbed vegetables languished in a half-filled bowl on the table between them, a dishtowel thrown over the top to ward off a pesky fly that had so far evaded Sam's whipping flyswatter.

"Listen to yourself. You're a reactionary and you aren't even forty," Hilary accused, then squinted across the table, studying the lines around his face. "Or are you?" He looked closer to thirty, but she'd enjoyed needling him this evening and parrying his return thrusts. She tried to predict his next words, but as usual, his closed expression offered no clues.

Slowly, a hint of a smile entered his eyes. It spread to his lips until a wide grin split his face from ear to ear. She felt as if the sun had just risen right there in the kitchen.

Even so, she couldn't resist one more jibe. "You find it amusing that you appear to be about forty?" she said.

He shook his head, still grinning. "When a woman

resorts to taunts about age, it generally means she's run out of reasonable arguments. You know I'm right. You just won't admit it."

"And when a man avoids the real issue, he knows he's lost. You're the one who's too stubborn to admit it," she replied.

"Actually, we'll both be dead before anyone knows who's really right," he said. He leaned across the table, his eyes trained somewhere to her left. Stretching the flyswatter ahead of him, he continued along the same line, drawing her attention back to his serious expression.

"Do computers help mankind or make destruction more efficient and organized?" he asked. "Are immunizations actually improving life by allowing millions of people to continue to overpopulate the world? I did a philosophy paper on that once as an undergrad. Got an A." His wrist flicked, and the loud whack of the flyswatter on the wall next to Hilary made her jump.

"Missed again," Sam muttered.

"In more ways than you realize. What about quality of life? Doesn't that count?" She snatched the swatter from his hand and flicked it on the front of the refrigerator. She eyed the nasty smear on the white, chipped enamel door. "Got it."

Sam stood up, the wide grin back in place. "Ben always said it's a good idea to let the woman win at something." He reached for his plate and set it in the sink, turning his back on her. A flush spread up the nape of his neck as he plugged the drain and squirted soap into the water.

"Sam?"

"Hmm?" The strangled sound was the only other clue she needed. He was laughing at her.

"Let the woman win?" she repeated, stepping

closer. When he nodded, still facing the window, she raised the swatter and flicked his backside.

He froze, then slowly turned to her with what was obviously meant to be a stern glare. But his eyes still crinkled at the corners with suppressed amusement.

"And what was that for?" he asked.

"For sexist, chauvinistic remarks and for evading the real issue. You're losing the argument and hunting for a diversion." She tossed the swatter out the door.

"What are you doing now?"

"Throwing my weapon outside so you can't use it against me. Let's get these dishes done before the sunlight fades completely. Otherwise, we'll have to turn on some modern lights powered by electricity produced in an environmentally hazardous process not available back in the good old days."

He rolled his eyes. "I'll wash." His dry tone made her wonder if she'd carried the argument a bit too far. Then, she caught the gleam of amused tolerance in his expression, as if he was humoring a particularly bright but fractious student. She grabbed up a towel, trying to think of a suitable response. When he flicked soap bubbles in her direction, she decided she must have mistaken his mood.

"No wonder you wanted to wash," she answered, throwing his own dryly amused expression back at him.

It should have taken about ten minutes to clean up the dinner dishes. But with sniping quips flying back and forth, occasionally accompanied by airborne clumps of dishsoap bubbles or a snapping towel, it took three times that long. Hilary finally had to turn on the overhead light.

"You missed some crumbs over there," Sam pointed out as she swept the insect and three of its friends into the dustpan he held.

She shrugged. "I'm trained in accounting and business, not sanitary engineering."

"That's garbage collection."

"Well, not that either," she said.

"In other words, nothing that gets your fingernails dirty," he taunted.

"That's not fair. A leaky ballpoint pen can really mess up a manicure," she teased.

He made a short, rude noise, but his eyes twinkled with laughter. "Quit playing with them and stay in the kitchen where women belong."

"That's a tacky remark." She turned away and tucked the dried plates into the open cabinet above her.

"Really tacky," he agreed. "Blame it on my Neanderthal tendencies." He pounded his chest, leaving wet blotches on his shirt.

Her laughter finally escaped. He really was priceless and completely unpredictable. How could he have known she needed to forget herself? She needed to argue, and be tacky and laugh at stupid jokes. He'd helped her regain her perspective.

Or maybe he didn't know. Maybe he needed the lightness more than she did. She sobered as she searched his face, seeing the shadows hovering at the edge of his smile. The laugh lines weren't that at all. They were lines of strain, deepened by the fright over the gas leak. He reminded her of her grandfather, and even her dad sometimes. Both covered their more serious emotions with laughter and jokes, playing at being strong and invulnerable.

"Neanderthals have their uses," she said softly.

He tilted his head, sobering at her changed tone. "Oh?" He pulled the sink plug and tossed it absently onto the counter. The sound of water gurgling down the drain hung between the two of them, filling the long silence. She swallowed hard at his warm, but wary look. "What uses?" he continued.

"Well," she began, drawing out the word while she considered. "Killing wild beasts. And building fires."

"And dragging foolish women out of danger," he finished for her.

He touched her chin briefly, then let his damp, dishwater finger trail along her jawline to the sensitive pulse point at its base. She'd never known warm water and lemon-scented dishsoap could be so seductive. Before she could think of a single intelligent thing to say, his hand dropped away. He picked up a serving bowl from the counter and lifted it into place on the high shelf behind her. He stood near enough to touch, but not touching her, as if leaving the next move to her.

She didn't feel crowded. She felt drawn, almost compelled to touch the firm expanse of his chest, the strong curve of his neck, the shaving nick she hadn't noticed before. When he backed away with nothing more than a muttered "excuse me," she wondered if she'd imagined the magnetic pull. No, it still tingled her tightly clenched fingers.

"You play checkers?" he asked as he stowed the dishpan and took the damp towel she still held.

Checkers? "Of course," she muttered faintly.

"Regular or King's Corner?" He hesitated. "Or cutthroat?"

Her gaze narrowed. He seemed so casual, so indifferent. She didn't know whether to be insulted or relieved.

"Choose your game and prepare to die," she answered, sweeping past him to clear the remaining condiments and the neatly folded newspaper from the center of the kitchen table. A good clean checkers match was exactly what she needed to remind herself that the two of them really weren't on the same side of anything, that they had nothing in common. She needed to beat him soundly.

By the time she'd stowed the clutter on the countertop, he'd set up the board. "You know the rules to Neill cutthroat?" he asked. "Ben and I used to play every Sunday."

"No holds barred, no limit on jumps, captures, kings, direction of movement, or prisoners of war."

"Prisoners of war?" He looked skeptical, the tolerant professor waiting for the student to hang herself with her own words. "That's a new twist. Explain, please."

"You ransom back captured pieces, negotiate for their release."

"And what is the ransom?"

Hilary shrugged. "It depends. Usually a trade, my captures for yours, with the men going back on the board at negotiated positions. Grandpa and I used to trade chores around the house. I got out of dishes for a month once, thanks to a cutthroat trade. I lost the game, but who cares about a game when the perks of losing are so good."

The professor look had disappeared, replaced by avid interest. "I should warn you that I've studied military strategy extensively," he said, making his first move with a bold nudge into a point position.

"Big deal. I have logic, mathematics, and statistics on my side. Besides, women are smarter, anyway. We only let you win sometimes to keep your male egos intact."

"Keep it up and you'll be cleaning my cave."

"In your dreams," she said, preparing to jump and capture his piece. He muttered something that sounded close to a groan. She couldn't tell whether it was in response to her retort or his incredibly stupid move. He stared intently at the board, then glanced up at her with challenge glittering within the warmth in his eyes.

She hesitated, sensing a trap.

"Your move," he prompted.

She glared. "When I'm ready. Or does Great Uncle Ben's version of cutthroat include a time limit?"

"Two minutes." The almost imperceptible shift in his expression was the only clue that he might be bluffing. She slipped off her sports watch, laying it on the table between them.

"Agreed."

Half an hour later, they were running even, with six men each left on the board and negotiations in progress for the prisoners of war.

"I'll trade you three commoners for a king right there," he said, pointing to an empty square next to one of her key men.

She leaned back, crossing her arms across her chest. "Do I look like a fool?"

Sam bent over the table, waggling his brows and flicking the ash from an imaginary cigar. "You're alone with me, my dear," he said in a blatant W.C. Fields imitation. Or was it Groucho Marx? She always got those old radio show routines confused.

"Isn't that a little modern for you?" she suggested.

"Yesterday is history, my dear."

She stared at the board, then turned a wide, cat-that-ate-the-canary smile on him. "Four commoners for the king," she offered.

That jarred his confidence. He pulled at his ear while studying the board. "You're up to something, aren't you?"

"You're the military strategist."

"You're bluffing," he charged.

Hilary crossed her toes and willed her smile to hold steady. "Try me."

He shook his head and pushed one of his six pieces

left on the board onto an adjoining square. "You're up to something."

She feigned innocence. "Don't you trust me?"

He leaned onto the table, his expression serious again. "I'm beginning to."

She knew by the lilt in his voice, the steadiness of his gaze, that he wasn't referring to the game. The sentiment warmed her, yet set her off-balance once again.

A loud chiming saved her from thinking of a suitable answer. The sound was reminiscent of old television sitcoms and melodramatic moments, the loud electric gonging of the pre-fab age.

"The doorbell," he said, not moving.

Hilary's brows arched meaningfully at the sound. "I suppose that was already here when you moved in."

"Of course. I'm thinking of replacing it with an old-fashioned authentic knocker." He pushed his chair back. Pure mischief gleamed in his chocolate eyes.

"Answer the door," she reminded him.

His gaze strayed reluctantly to the checkerboard and winced. His last move had been suicidal, setting himself up for a double capture. And as far as she could tell, he could do nothing to stop it or retaliate. It gave her a moderate thrill, she decided. He'd been distracted enough by their argument, by her, to forget strategy. He might even have been flirting in a roundabout way. And she was woman enough to appreciate it, even though she knew she shouldn't.

"You go ahead," she said. "I'll just sit here and plan my next move."

"It shouldn't take long. Probably somebody asking for directions, or—" He slapped his palm against his forehead. "Damn, I know who it is."

He rushed out of the room, muttering something beneath his breath. Intrigued, she followed him. She hesitated in the doorway to the central hall, hanging back in the shadows of the darkened room. Sam cast an undecipherable look in her direction, then swung the front door wide.

"There you are, boy. The missus and I had just about decided you weren't home." The tall booming voice didn't seem to match the slight, elderly man who entered the house, gesturing with a long, knobby stick that Hilary decided must be a homemade cane. His clothes seemed from another era, not the dated, frugal look common among the elderly, but from another century altogether.

A well-padded woman in long-skirted calico swished briskly in behind him and grabbed the cane a split second before it crashed against the antique brass light fixture hanging above them.

"And we were going to leave a note," she said, not missing a beat as she leaned the cane against the wall. Her voice was deeper than her husband's, with the faint, hoarse rasp that men seemed to find sexy in much younger women.

"Since you're here," she continued, "we can tell you in person. Why weren't you at the volunteers meeting, anyway? We could have used your support against that sour-faced director and her nitpicky rules. She's forbidden Melvin from wearing his red longjohns at the park. As if it's anybody's business what he wears underneath it all. So long as the rest is authentic 1855, what does it matter?"

"Well," Sam began in a conciliatory tone. "The red union suits don't date back quite that far."

"As if anyone would know the difference," the woman retorted.

Sam cleared his throat and cast a helpless, apologetic look at Hilary. It was all the encouragement she needed to join them. He seemed in need of rescue from the garrulous older couple. They must be some of the re-enactors he worked with at the nearby living history park, she surmised. More nuts who liked playing dress-up, though they appeared to be nice enough.

He sidestepped her way and clasped her hand, drawing her under the circle of light cast by the antique fixture. "Mr. and Mrs. Chandler, meet Hilary Neill, the new owner of Neill House. She's come to go through Ben's papers and sort out a few details while she decides what to do with the property. Perhaps you can help me persuade her to our way of thinking," he said, leaning close like a conspirator about to lay out a plan. His broad wink only strengthened the effect. "She's as stubborn as the rest of the Neills, though."

Hilary barely contained the impulse to roll her eyes and laugh at the theatrics. "Good evening," she said, holding out her hand. "Sam and I were finishing a game of checkers."

The woman looked faintly skeptical as she took Hilary's hand in a bone-crunching grasp. "It's lovely to finally meet you, dear. I'd wondered . . . well, never mind. Are you just here for another visit or are you planning to stay?"

"Oh, leave the girl be, Rosemary." Her husband's grip, in turn, was only slightly less vigorous.

"We didn't mean to interrupt your game. We'll only stay a minute," Mrs. Chandler said.

Sam flicked a wall switch and flooded the living room with the faintly yellow light of incandescent bulbs shining through old fixtures and a film of dust. His eyes seemed paler than in the fluorescent light of the kitchen—a tawny color that reminded Hilary of a big, watching puma, content for now to observe and taunt with an occasional soft growl.

"Please stay," he begged the Chandlers. "She prefers Ben's cutthroat version of checkers, only with a few vicious twists added in.''

The old man brightened. "That's where I remember you from. I believe I saw you at the funeral, didn't I? Not Ben's, but a few years ago when—'' he hesitated, glancing contritely at Sam. "Anyway, that's the first time any of us had seen Robert in twenty years or more. I had hoped he'd stay around a bit longer. There's not too many of us left from the old Cyclone Road schoolyard.''

Hilary stopped abruptly on her way to the settee in the corner. "You knew Grandpa?"

Mr. Chandler snorted, drawing a disapproving frown from his wife. "Knew him? Heck, girl, I got into more trouble with those two Neill brothers than I ever did on my own. What one didn't think of, the other did.''

"Melvin Chandler, you do tend to exaggerate," his wife interjected with an indulgent tap on his shoulder. "Don't forget I knew the three of you then as well as now. You were definitely the worst of the lot.''

The old man ignored her. "Didn't he ever tell you about the time we rode Old Man Neill's—that's your granddaddy's granddaddy—anyway, we rode his horse through the schoolhouse on Christmas morning. The old man would've tanned our hides with that big black whip he used on the mules—if he could've caught us.'' He winked in Hilary's direction. "Had to camp out in the woods for three days.''

"I suppose you had to come home sometime," Hilary answered, remembering the one and only time she'd run away from home herself. Her mother had reminded her of that fact as she had left the house. Her rebellion had lasted a half-hour, then she'd quietly returned to the restaurant kitchen and to work. Nothing more had been said, and she'd never repeated the experience.

"You did come home, didn't you?" she continued,

turning to Mr. Chandler and noting the twinkling glint in the man's pale-blue eyes.

"You had to ask," Sam said.

Mr. Chandler shoved up his shirt sleeves and sank heavily onto the deep cushions of the overstuffed sofa. His wife balked when he patted the cushion beside him.

"Really, Melvin. I doubt the girl has much interest in what three ornery boys were up to sixty-seven years ago—"

"Sixty-eight," Melvin interjected. "It was right after my eleventh birthday."

"She's probably heard that story and all the others enough times already to be thoroughly bored with the subject," Mrs. Chandler continued. "Besides, we need to get home."

"What for? Nothin' to do except watch the blamed television and go to bed and stare at the ceiling in the dark for a couple of hours. Might as well sit here in the light as do that." He pointed a bony finger at Sam. "Don't ever retire, boy. Biggest mistake I ever made. Even bigger mistake than marrying a bossy woman."

Mrs. Chandler leaned over and placed a loud kiss on the man's forehead. "It's a trial, isn't it? Hilary, be warned, once he starts he doesn't stop until he falls asleep or his audience does." A warm look passed between the older couple as she settled onto the couch beside him.

"Do you have time?" Mr. Chandler asked, uncertainty flickering briefly across the wrinkled folds of his rawboned face.

Hilary glanced at Sam, uncertain whether to humor the old man or manufacture a task to attend to. It was Sam's house, after all, and his neighbors. His nonchalant shrug told her nothing, but the glint in his cat eyes played havoc with her breathing once again. She decided she was too susceptible to his brand of charm to remain alone with him for long.

"Grandpa never said much about growing up here or why he left," she said, returning her earnest gaze to Mr. Chandler. "I didn't even know he had a brother until several years ago. He never wanted to talk about his family."

"That would be because of what happened later," Mr. Chandler said. "But as I was saying—"

"Maybe Miss Neill would rather hear why Bob left."

The twinkling faded. "Who's telling the stories here? She doesn't want to hear about that mess now. It'd keep her up all night, just thinking about it." He swiveled to face Hilary, putting her on the spot. "I'm right, aren't I? But you do need to know what kind of trouble boys can get themselves into, in case you're thinking of having any of your own. You might change your mind." The wink returned, broader this time, leaving her in little doubt as to the efficiency of the local grapevine concerning her marital status—and probably every other detail down to the size of her shoes.

She couldn't help grinning at the predictability of it all. "I haven't done anything irreversible in that quarter yet," she said.

Chandler's hand slapped hard on his knee. "That didn't tell me a blamed thing. Spoken like a true Neill, wouldn't you say so, Sam? Not only does she look like 'em, she talks like 'em."

Sam's glance was more speculative than amused. Hilary contained the urge to squirm under his gaze. Instead, she returned his stare with practiced stillness.

"I have noticed certain tendencies that remind me of the family," he said.

She thought she detected a hint of approval in his

tone. A step closer to acceptance, she translated silently with an unreasonably strong surge of pleasure.

"We didn't come here to hash over the family skeletons with the poor girl. We came here to tell Sam about that nonsense at the meeting," Mrs. Chandler reminded him.

"In good time, woman," her husband retorted good naturedly. "Right now, I've more important things to talk about."

Mrs. Chandler's tolerant smirk indicated this was an old routine. "I'll make coffee" was all she said as she turned toward the kitchen, her long skirts swishing with each brisk step.

"As I was saying . . ." Mr. Chandler continued, rubbing his knee in an unconscious gesture that hinted at chronic pain. "Me and the Neill boys were hiding down in the bottoms along the creek. That was long before the Corps put in the lake and that whole area became the county park."

His voice wrapped Hilary in the spell woven by a natural storyteller as he recounted the adventures of those three days in the woods. The story flowed into another and more after that.

Some moments later, Sam left the door frame he'd been leaning against and cut across the room toward the settee. Hilary moved over to make room for him, hugging the arm while trying to appear at ease. The storyteller's spell was broken. In truth, her every nerve ending screamed at Sam's nearness. She wished he'd pulled a chair in from the kitchen or taken the oak swivel at the desk. Silly, maybe, but she'd be more comfortable with him across the room. Or maybe not. At least she couldn't see those cat eyes watching her anymore. She forced her attention back to the storyteller, ignoring the prickling rise of the hair on her arm next to his.

In the close quiet of the old house, with the old man's mesmerizing voice and the steady, loud tick of the big regulator clock, her tenseness slowly faded into true ease. Too close became a comfortable nearness.

"And we stuffed those chickens, all twenty-four of them, into the outhouse," Melvin continued.

Hilary released an indelicate snort. "You're pulling my leg. The plumbing at Neill House predates the Great Chicago Fire. Why would they have an outhouse, too?"

"You don't think Mrs. Neill let a bunch of dirty farmworkers or snot-nosed kids into her shiny white room, do you?"

Mrs. Chandler nodded, a resigned expression on her face. "It's mostly true, dear."

"As I was saying, when the foreman opened the door, out comes that big banty rooster, flapping his wings and spurring anything he bumped into. And the others were nearly as crazy. . . ." Mr. Chandler went on.

Hilary lost the rest. Sam shifted beside her, reawakening the sharp awareness of her lulled senses. The old settee creaked beneath them as he stretched an arm across the back, not touching her but near enough for her to feel the heat radiating from his skin. The hair at the nape of her neck felt as if it were standing at attention, tensing for his touch.

Suddenly, she became aware of the silence as Mr. Chandler paused for a long drink of coffee. Fortunately, he hadn't seemed to notice that her attention had wandered.

"Were you still friends with my grandfather and his brother when you were older?" she asked.

"To the end," he declared with a sad expression.

"I'm sorry. I guess what I'm asking is why my grandfather left. I've been trying to figure it out since I learned about Great Uncle Ben and all of that."

Mr. Chandler shook his head. "You'll have to ask Rosemary that one. It's more her story than mine."

Puzzled, Hilary looked to the older woman. "It's long and complicated. For now, I'll just say that there was a disagreement over a woman."

"I can't imagine what else would split apart two brothers as close as that," her husband added gruffly, then spoiled the effect with another of his winks. "Except Rosemary's sister."

"What happened?" Hilary asked.

Mr. Chandler tapped his blunt nails against the saucer while he considered. "Go on and tell it, Rosemary. But don't drag it out with all your sighs and heart patterings."

The woman shot him a dark look. "The short version then. Hilary, your grandfather was in love with my sister, Edith, but it seemed as if they could never get any time alone because when their parents and aunts and uncles and so forth weren't watching them, Ben was tagging along and keeping them straight.

"Well, the two of them got engaged and set the wedding date. Ben caused all kinds of trouble, because, you see, he wanted Edith himself. And it seems he wanted her more than he wanted to stay on good terms with his brother. So, he started courting her, trying to turn her head away from Bob. Two weeks before the wedding, Edith changed her mind and decided she wanted Ben instead. So Ben, having been in love with her all along, stepped right into his brother's place and married her. Bob caused a terrible commotion at the wedding and they had to lock him out of the church. A real scandal," she said, her eyes flashing with delight. "The next day, he took off for parts unknown and nobody heard from him for two years. And he didn't put a foot back on the Neill place until the day you came with him."

"I don't guess he ever forgave any of us for locking him out, but that's what Edith asked us to do and so—" Mr. Chandler paused as the regulator clock chimed the hour of eleven.

"Is it that late?" he said, his eyes seeking Sam for confirmation. "Or did you forget to wind and reset it again?"

"It definitely is late," his wife confirmed after a glance at the watch tucked into a hidden pocket. "Finish this story and then we'd best be going."

The old man stood, dismissing the suggestion with a wave of his hand. "Gotta give the girl a reason to invite us up to the house, both of us, once she's all settled in," he said. "Now, where's my cane?"

Mrs. Chandler pushed herself to her feet and exchanged a knowing smile with Sam. This, too, was apparently part of the routine.

She turned her smile on Hilary and pulled her into a quick, unexpected hug that was over before she had time to react. "I'm glad there's still some of the Neill family around," Mrs. Chandler said. "Have you found the family portraits yet? I think Ben put them in the attic while he was working on the parlor. Never got around to bringing them back down."

"Now that I know about the pictures I'll have to hunt for them," Hilary answered, feeling a bit unsteady from the sudden show of affection.

"Please do. You look so much like Ben and like Sarah, too, don't you think, Sam? She has the same hair, only short—and the same general face. Those Neill genes are strong, aren't they?"

Hilary tried to smile, but she couldn't shrug off her discomfort as her glance shifted to Sam. The comparison to his dead wife made her uncomfortable, even though he showed no sign of the same unease. Instead, he met her gaze steadily with a rising heat that danced on top of her misgivings, tamping them down, and confusing them with stronger, more clearly defined feelings. Dangerous feelings.

Oblivious to the undercurrents she had set free, Mrs. Chandler bustled about helping her husband. "Hilary, I didn't see your car in the driveway. Can we give you a ride over to the house?"

Again, Sam's eyes darkened with warning. "That's all right," he said before she could speak. "We need to finish our game."

"It's terribly late. The poor girl looks tired," Mrs. Chandler argued, stifling a yawn herself.

Sam smiled wickedly. "Then I have a chance at winning after all." He held the door wide, then walked with the older couple to the car, chatting about the incident that sent them hurrying here in the first place. Hilary hung back, distancing herself from the cozy intimacy. She wasn't a part of their group and didn't want to intrude.

Sam returned almost immediately, and the Chandlers' tail lights soon lit a red path down the drive and around the corner of the blacktop.

"They're nice," Hilary commented, stepping back inside. "Interesting, too. I hope you weren't bored. You've probably heard the stories before."

"Dozens of times, but tonight was different."

"How's that?" She headed into the next room and picked up the coffee tray with its empty pot and dirty cups.

"They weren't just an old man's stories. I watched your face. You were soaking up clues, hints of how your grandfather came to be the man he was."

She smiled wistfully up at Sam. "I still miss him. I wish it was him telling the stories. I wish he could have told me years ago." She turned away, not wanting him to see the tears welling up in her eyes. Funny, she hadn't cried in months. It was the stories. They'd made her miss her grandpa more than ever.

She set the tray beside the sink and reached for the hot water faucet handle. Sam's hand closed over hers before she could twist it on. "Leave it."

"It'll only take a minute." She hated the quaver in her voice, the lump in her throat. Most of all, she hated the heat seeping from his hand into hers, stealing up her arm to wrap itself around her heart. She ought to pull away, but just now she didn't have the will to resist it.

She turned to face him. "I should go home now."

He caught her chin, holding her still with the barest of touches. "Not a chance. And I won't take you to a hotel, either."

"And when the Chandlers hear about the gas leak? You know they will. What will they think?"

"Why should it matter to you? You're a big-city woman, just here for a vacation until you go back to your real life."

She backed away from his touch. His hand hovered in the air where her chin had been, then dropped slowly to his side and tapped restlessly against the nearby chair back.

"I like them," she said. "I don't want them to get the wrong idea. I don't want to offend them."

"You're engaged. You even came down here with your fiancé. That should protect your reputation with the locals should word get out that you spent the night here. Besides, I'm not exactly the local Lothario."

"You sound so Victorian. I'm not that worried about my reputation." His sudden gallantry would be amusing, if he wasn't so serious about it.

He hesitated, then took a step closer. "I told them about the leak. They offered their spare room."

"And you didn't tell me or give me a chance to make my own decision. You told them that I'd—" Indignation replaced all trace of amusement. "That's as much as saying—well, as saying . . .'' She sputtered on the last words, then crossed her arms and glared at him.

''What?'' He came even closer. ''That I wanted to keep an eye on you for a while—that I'm still trying to figure something out.''

''Oh?'' She threw all the frost she could manage into the single syllable.

His hands settled on her stiff shoulders. ''It's not just circumstances. There's more than *déjà vu* and circumstances and the dominant Neill genes at work here.''

''You're imagining it.''

He shook his head, his tawny eyes deepening to near black as they seemed to swallow her. ''Something's happening here. Don't you want to know what?''

She backed up, bumping against the wall. The flyswatter hook hung bare above her. She wished she hadn't thrown the blasted thing outside. She needed every weapon she could muster to fight this attraction between them. But she had none at her disposal except steadfast denial and the fading image of Kyle in her mind. Kyle with his disapproving frown and his steamroller approach to life. Sam was pushing her, too, but he left the choices to her.

''I already told you—it's just circumstances,'' she insisted.

''You'll always wonder. Why not find out?''

Her eyes narrowed. ''Exactly what are you suggesting?''

He held up his hand and slowly closed his fingers against his palm, all except one. ''A kiss. One single kiss. If you don't feel anything, we'll both know you were right.''

She bit her lip, considering his proposal. ''A test, huh?'' She hadn't expected such a logical approach.

She couldn't argue with the sense of it, only the danger of it.

"Are you afraid I'm right?"

"Don't be ridiculous!"

He watched her with those magical eyes. "You're tempted, aren't you? You want to know as much as I do."

She turned away. "Don't flatter yourself." He was making too much sense, though. She didn't want to resist, torn as she was with her own questions and doubts.

"Prove me wrong."

"All right," she said, uncrossing her arms and leaning up on tiptoe. She could do this. She had to. She had to know.

He met her halfway, maybe more than halfway. It didn't matter because the instant his lips touched hers, the embers sparked and kindled. Soft, yet humming with vibrant life like all her senses. She could feel his breath fanning her face, smell the sweetness of it, taste the faint hint of tomato that lingered from dinner.

It wasn't like the first kiss, born of fear and instinct. This was the two of them with nothing else to blame for the feelings coursing between them. And that made it all the more irresistible.

His lips seduced hers, touching with whisper softness, then retreating, forcing hers to follow or suffer a bereftness beyond bearing. Her arms stole around his neck, pulling him closer as he abandoned her mouth for the sensitive side of her neck, the tender spot behind her ear. A shiver trembled through her. She heard a sharply drawn gasp, then realized it was her own.

With a deep groan, he circled her in his arms and crushed her against him. His lips abandoned their teasing and closed over hers with a passion that fed her own. A white-hot ball of heat knotted in her belly, then swelled and spread. She leaned against him, clutching at his shoulders to keep her knees from buckling. He touched the very bedrock of her being. She was lost in him and she didn't even care.

While his mouth roamed freely, his hands rested at her shoulders, stroking and massaging, yet glued to that one spot with restless control. Her boundaries were not so constrained. She explored the feel of him, the taste of him and revelled in each sensation. Her fingers caressed his neck, wrapped in his silky hair, then danced along the muscles of his arms only to abandon them to wrap herself around him, against him. And when she thought she could no longer breathe, that she no longer needed to, he lifted his head and touched a trembling finger to the racing pulse at the base of her throat. The tender gesture set off another trembling wave that was frightening in its intensity.

Hilary leaned against the wall, shaken. "I'm in big trouble," she whispered, surprised she could speak at all.

"I think we both are." He traced the line of her jaw with the back of his outstretched hand. "I'm not sure yet what to do about it."

"Nothing," she said. "We do nothing."

"Maybe. For now." He stepped aside.

"I need to think." She didn't really. She already knew what she had to do. She only had to figure out the when and how of it.

"Maybe we both need to. The trouble is, I'm not sure I can right now. Maybe after a good night's sleep."

Hilary nodded. That's what she needed, a good night's sleep. Everything would be clearer in the morning. She hoped the old axiom was true, because she'd certainly landed herself in a muddle tonight.

"I'll show you to your room." He stood back, not even trying to touch her now. He didn't need to. He'd proved his point, and so very thoroughly. But he didn't look as if it had made him happy. The shadows behind the smile hadn't disappeared.

SEVEN

The long, eerie howl ended with a sharp yip that ripped through Hilary's restless dream. She awoke with a sharp jerk and stared shakily around the room, searching the shadows for whatever had awakened her. She'd recognized the sound, but she didn't know if it was real or she'd dreamed it.

Her heart throbbed in her throat as she fought off the disorientation of the strange room, where everything seemed in the wrong place, even rearranged since she'd turned off the light only hours before. Closing her eyes, she took a deep, steadying breath and counted to ten before exhaling. It was always like this when she awoke suddenly in an unfamiliar place.

Slowly, her heart stopped thudding so loudly in her ears and allowed other sounds to seep in. Unfamiliar night sounds. The hoot of an owl, the plaintive howl of a coyote, some loud screeching that sounded like geese. The house itself was silent except for the occasional creaks that all old houses make. No footsteps in the hall or whisper of movement indicated Sam had been disturbed by the cacophony outside. But why should he be? These sounds must be as familiar to him as the sirens, backfires, and passing car radios of her own neighborhood back in Chicago were to her.

Hilary glanced around the room, identifying each shadow in turn. The coyote concert resumed in rondo—all howling the same part but never starting at the same time—until Hilary could no longer tell when one beast's song began and another's ended. "Row, Row, Row Your Boat" for canines. The din fed the restlessness that had kept her tossing and turning since she'd first laid her head on the pillow in Sam's guest room.

"It doesn't make sense," she whispered in the dark for the tenth time that night.

Take this room—the casual clutter of the rest of the house was missing. It was spotless, dustless, with clothesline-fresh sheets, and floors polished to a high sheen. The furniture tops were as barren as those of a hotel. Nothing adorned the walls except the blue, fine-print wallpaper, which appeared much newer than the faded paper in the rest of the house.

But it was more than that. It was the way he'd lingered at the doorway, looking past her with such far-away shadows in his eyes. There was something odd about this room, something she couldn't quite put her finger on. It was as if someone had just moved out.

She tried again to puzzle it out. It distracted her from her own problems and the unsettling dream she'd awakened from. She couldn't recall anything specific, just a general sense of confusion and unfocused energy. Even now, when she was awake, she couldn't stay still.

Maybe some milk would help. Wasn't there some naturally occurring chemical in milk that helped induce peaceful sleep? Or was it just another old story that mothers and grandmothers told children to scare away their nightmares?

Might as well try it, she thought as she untangled

her legs from the twisted top sheet and stretched her feet over the edge of the tall four-poster. Stepping quietly so she wouldn't disturb Sam, she tiptoed across the polished-wood floor and slipped her jeans back on under her borrowed, oversized T-shirt.

The door swung easily on well-oiled hinges and only one stair creaked, so she managed her descent to the main floor in relative silence. The moonlight shining between the opened curtains was so bright she didn't need to turn on any lights. She'd just poured a tall glass of cold milk when a rhythmic buzzing began. Crickets. She chuckled at the sound. At least she was used to crickets. They grew big and loud in the city, too.

She drank the milk in a rush, not caring for the taste. Of course, folklore had it that the milk must be warm to work the cure. But drinking it cold was bad enough. Drinking it warm was out of the question. She set the glass in the sink and ran water into it, glancing outside again and remembering how she'd watched covertly from behind these same curtains earlier.

The muted screech of a goose drew her attention from the fire pit and the remembered picture of Sam leaning over it, testing the coals and turning the meat. Out by the garden, a figure balanced in eerie concentration atop a fencepost. For an instant, she thought her imagination was playing another joke on her conscious mind. Then she realized the figure perched on the fence post was as real as her own flesh and blood.

Sitting there, his heels hooked around the fence rungs and his face silhouetted in profile by the moon behind him, he looked like a fairy-tale warlock silently gathering his power for his next spell. Or a shirtless warrior seeking a vision. He looked alone, apart, but not lonely. Just solemn and otherworldly.

The back door was unlocked, of course. How else could a flesh-and-blood warlock have escaped from the house? She padded silently across the porch, down the steps, and into the grass, her gaze alternating between her footing and the unmoving figure in the moon. *The man in the moon. Her man in the moon.* She shook her head, laughing to herself at such ridiculous ramblings. Even so, she recognized in her silence an instinctive, superstitious fear that sometimes escaped after midnight, with or without the help of the moon. *What if. . . ?*

The sensible, pragmatic part of her didn't believe it, though. Her step lightened as she scrunched the soft grass between her toes and sidestepped a thistle at the last instant. A quarter of the way, then half, and still he hadn't moved at all.

A small animal cry, chilling as a woman's scream, though not so loud, drifted over from the darkness of the woods beyond the barn. The sound raised goose bumps all over her body. Hilary froze and considered the merits of returning to the enclosed safety of the house.

"It's only a fox, a vixen calling to her mate." Sam's voice dispelled any mystical illusions, even if he didn't stop the night sounds. The fox called again, and Hilary couldn't contain a shudder at the sound. Giving it a name didn't make it any less creepy.

She walked quickly over to the fence and leaned against the top rail. "I didn't mean to disturb you," she said, then wished she could take the inane words back. She should have stayed indoors.

"The geese were squawking about something."

"I heard." His feet were bare like hers, with neatly trimmed toenails and a few coarse hairs sprinkled on the toes and instep. They matched the sprinkling on his chest. Good grief, she had it so badly she was developing a foot fetish.

"The fox or the coyotes?" she continued.

"Or maybe a fight over a particularly big bug," he

said with a low chuckle. "I'll put them in the barn just in case."

"You do take the romance out of a moonlit night," she answered with a rueful laugh of her own. "I think I'll go back in before you destroy all my illusions."

"You don't have to go," he said. "I was just sitting out here, enjoying the occasional breeze and thinking about things."

She leaned back onto the fence. "What things?"

"Oh, nothing much. Lesson plans for next week, the wattle fence I'm building up at the park, the meaning of life . . ." He laughed again, though confusion lay beneath the lightness. He had his own puzzles to sort out. Maybe the kisses had disturbed him, too. Maybe he really believed there was something between them. Her heart lurched at the thought.

"Maybe it's the humidity," she offered. "I haven't slept well tonight either."

His look was dubious. "Maybe. I could turn the air conditioner back on. It doesn't do much good for the second floor, but you're welcome to the couch."

A brief mental picture of the lumpy, sagging relic flashed through Hilary's mind. "Thanks, but I'll make do with the guest room. It's beautiful, by the way."

He nodded. "Sarah redecorated it right after we were married. She was good with colors, fabrics, textures, you know—artsy things."

Hilary had to smile at his description. "I thought she was a musician, piano wasn't it?"

"Mostly, though she had a guitar she used to play sometimes. She was very artistic in other ways, too, always painting or stitching something. She did your dining-room chair seats."

"My chairs?" Then it hit her. Ben's dining room. She just wasn't used to thinking of it as hers, maybe because she hadn't really lived in the house yet. She hadn't even decided whether to keep it or try to break the deed restriction.

I could keep it.

"The chairs are beautiful," she said. "I didn't realize Sarah had so many talents. I wish I could have known her."

She did, truly. She wished the accident had never killed the relatives she'd never been allowed to meet. In that case, though, she'd be having unacceptable thoughts about a married man. But that scenario would be simpler than the one she faced now. The line between black and white wouldn't be blurred into gray smudges.

"She would have liked you," Sam said, touching Hilary's hair.

She gulped, willing herself not to lean into his touch. She couldn't, not when the ghost of Sarah was so much with them, so much in his thoughts. Not when she hadn't untied her own commitments.

"I would have liked her, too," Hilary managed. Her throat choked with emotion, barely letting the words slip past. "The piano?"

"I had it moved back to Ben's. I couldn't look at it. And he wanted it," he explained.

"Then I have it now," she said. "If you want—"

"Keep it," he interrupted, sincerity humming in his low tones. He took her hands, gripping them between his warm, solid palms. "It's a beautiful baby grand. It always looked out of place here. The rooms are too small. Besides, Sarah's been gone a long time. It's just a piano now."

Hilary nodded because that's all she was capable of for a moment. Seven years was a long time, she reasoned. And it had been seven years—long enough for the memories to lose their sharp edge. The pain of the pale young man she'd met when she was an even younger woman had eased to bittersweet twinges. She wondered whether moonlight made them better or worse.

He squeezed her hands, then released them. "Life goes on," he said with a shrug. "Ben taught me that and he showed me how. I owe the old man a lot."

"We Neills are pretty smart," she said in an attempt at lightness.

His brows lifted skeptically. "The older ones, maybe. It remains to be seen whether this generation lives up to the legacy," he said.

Hilary didn't need to ask what he meant. She knew. He'd used the same tone every time he'd referred to Kyle. She had her own doubts, but she wasn't about to admit them now, not to Sam. The situation between them was too volatile already.

"Aren't you afraid the geese will eat everything?" she said, changing the subject.

He let the tactic pass with scarcely more than a knowing smile. "I plant enough for all of us," he said. "Me and the geese, that is. Mostly they eat the bugs and the corn I throw out. They don't do too much damage. The deer are the real problem."

"Why don't you get a dog?"

"I had one. She died a couple of months ago. Old age."

Hilary nodded. "You miss her?"

"Some. Mostly, I don't want to worry about training a puppy right now. I'm gone too much."

"Hmm. Maybe you'd be home more if you had some company here," she argued.

"Are you offering?"

"I was talking about the puppy."

"Right. I thought so," he replied in a tone that implied the opposite. Hilary felt like slugging him. Instead, she changed the subject again.

"What's a waffle fence?"

"A what?"

"You said you were building one at the park."

"Oh, a wattle fence. It's made of sticks woven together. Mostly it's for chicken yards and the like. It predates chicken wire by a couple thousand years, and the materials are as readily available as trees," he explained.

"Neanderthal chicken wire?"

He chuckled. "You are incorrigible. I'm not letting you anywhere near any of my students. You're a bad influence."

"Maybe," she admitted, stifling an unexpected yawn. "I'd better go in. I'll see you in the morning."

"Sleep as late as you like," he said.

She smiled sleepily as she turned toward the house. "Hilary?"

She paused, looking up at him. "Yes?"

"We'll both find our answers," he said. His confidence filled her, making her believe, too. "It may take some time, but we'll figure it all out and make something worth keeping out of it."

The words cut through the pretense and the defenses she'd erected to hide her thoughts. He'd said nothing and everything. Earlier, his eyes had made love to her. Now, they promised more.

The knowledge didn't strike her as a hot jolt of electricity, but as a slow, spreading warmth that sent waves of pleasure throughout her body. She knew then he'd be the one she could not forget, the one she'd remember when she was an old woman, telling her grandchildren tales of her romances before she met their grandfather.

For an instant, her soul had smiled at his. And this time he hadn't even touched her.

"Good night," she mouthed, though no sound escaped. She ran across the yard and onto the porch.

When she glanced back from the back door, she saw him again, silhouetted against the moon as she'd found him. A few minutes later, she glanced out again, this time from the bedroom window. He was gone. Then she saw him, shooing the geese out of the garden and around the corner of the barn.

She glanced around the room. It had been *their* room, the one Sarah had decorated and the only one she'd had time to finish. Their room, their marriage bed. And she knew instinctively that Sam hadn't slept in it for seven years.

She crawled on top of the sheets and hugged her pillow. She didn't have her answers yet, not all of them. But she wasn't worried about them anymore. Sam said he'd moved on. Just as she had to.

The back door clicked shut, the faint sound drifting up to the second story. Then Sam's barefoot tread creaked on the staircase. He walked carefully, as if trying not to awaken her. As if she could sleep.

He paused outside her door, and she held her breath. For one terrifying, exhilarating instant, she thought he would turn the knob and come inside. Then he moved on.

"Good night, Hilary," he murmured, his voice soft and warm.

"Good night," she answered.

The footfalls stopped, then resumed as a light, surprised laugh drifted down the hall. And Hilary got the distinct impression that he hadn't expected her to hear him.

The sun shone bright and hot through the open window when Hilary finally awoke. The smell of coffee teased her groggy senses, and she thought she heard a jaunty whistle coming from down the hall. A door opened, the whistle got louder, and light, squeaky sneaker steps passed by her door. She rubbed her eyes and groaned. It was morning. Heck, it had been morning when she'd gone back to sleep. The sun just hadn't known it yet.

Men who whistle in the morning should be shot before they bother anyone.

She dragged her protesting limbs out of bed and down the hall to the bathroom. She'd just rinse her face, comb her hair, and then think about getting dressed. If she could find a comb.

She could barely find the bathroom, even though she'd been there the night before. The toilet paper presented a fresh, new challenge, but finally it appeared on the wall dispenser. The fool thing had probably been there all along. She tried rinsing her face, but it didn't refresh her as it usually did. Worse yet, the whistling continued, still louder. It sounded suspiciously like *Eine kleine nachtmusik.* Imagine being able to whistle Mozart, in the morning, no less. She couldn't hum a recognizable tune when she was wide awake.

She glanced out the tiny window and spotted Sam on the way back to the house, newspaper in hand. He waved, dropping Mozart for a low wolf whistle. She slammed the window shut, ignoring the flush his attention brought. No man had the right to be that charming or that cheerful in the morning, not on so little sleep.

Ten minutes later, after a teeth-chattering shower and a brisk towel rub, she felt much more alive. She wriggled back into the T-shirt and scurried down the hall for the safety of her room. Wide awake, she was much more conscious of her bare state beneath the shirt, not to mention the way the damp neckline clung to her.

By the time she'd dressed and used his blow-dryer, she was in a more forgiving mood. She could even tolerate the whistling, she decided, noting that Sam had switched from Mozart to nursery songs, which required considerably less finesse. She'd also heard two sour notes. They made her feel right at home. So did the delicious smells wafting through the house.

"What's for breakfast?" she asked as she breezed through the kitchen doorway, straight for the coffeepot. A little caffeine would bolster the bounce she'd forced into her step. Her hand paused in midair as she caught sight of Sam's drab, worn clothes and frayed suspenders.

"Corn pone and grits?" she suggested with a straight face. She concentrated on pouring her coffee, barely managing to contain a giggle. In those clothes, he looked like one of old Mr. Chandler's hired hands. Sam must be working up at the living history park today.

"How witty, Ms. Neill. Sausage, eggs, biscuits, and gravy," Sam said. He stood in front of the stove, stirring the last with a practiced hand. He adjusted the flame, then pointed out the newspaper stacked neatly between two place settings. "Have a seat. The business section is on top."

Hilary hesitated, tapping the counter restlessly. "I'm on vacation," she reminded him.

He shrugged. "Read the funnies. Just don't mess with the crossword puzzle."

Hilary shot him a surprised look. "I never would have taken you for a crossword fanatic."

"I'm saving them for my Great-Aunt Ethel," he said, studying the gravy. When he looked up, a mischievous twinkle sparkled in the warm brown eyes.

"Whatever you say, Langford" was her only response as she settled into her chair.

"Hey, I'll tolerate no disrespect in my kitchen," he said. He pulled two covered bowls out of the oven and set them on the table. "Now, eat."

Hilary leaned over, lifting a lid to peer dubiously at

the scrambled mess of yellow, red, and various hues in between. "What's that?"

"Scrambled eggs and tomatoes."

"Oh." She reached for the biscuits.

"You're the one who picked them. You don't expect me to let them go to waste now, do you?"

Hilary gamely added a spoonful of the egg concoction to her plate. She had to. He would be unbearable if she turned up her nose at it and didn't even taste it.

The thought came as easily as the assumption that they'd spend more time together, that he enjoyed her company as much as she liked his. Actually, she might not see him again for her entire visit. The idea tainted her appetite more than the sight of the egg mess. She shoveled a forkful into her mouth.

No, she knew she'd see him. Last night's kiss had told her that much.

"What are you doing today?" he asked.

She glared at him. Trust a man to start a conversation when the woman's mouth was full of food and her head was full of doubts.

"By the way, the plumber's already up at the house. He thinks he found the leak."

Hilary swallowed. "Wonderful. I suppose you've already been up to Neill House, too."

He nodded. "We were right. The break is right next to the waterline repair."

"Did he say when he'd be finished?"

"Sometime next week. He has to order some fittings. You'll need to talk to him before he leaves."

"Fine. I'm going home now, anyway," she said. She half-expected him to challenge her, even now.

The idea didn't seem to bother him at all. "The gas is all cleared out. We checked already."

"That's good to know." She reached for the eggs to cover her disquiet. "These aren't half bad," she added.

He didn't say I told you so, not in so many words. He could speak much more succinctly with a pointed look. She'd just bet that look worked even better on his freshman class.

"I'll be tied up most of the day over at the park," he said a few moments later. "Maybe this evening we could check the attic for those family pictures."

She grinned across the table at him. "There's one package of sauerbraten left in the freezer. Want to share it?"

His smile matched hers, then added sparks of fire. "You bet."

"Six o'clock."

"I'll bring the wine," he said with a wicked wink. A wave of heat flowed straight across the table and stole her breath.

She picked up the paper, hiding her reaction. She stared blindly at the page until he exclaimed at the time and hurried off with a quick kiss on her forehead.

So domestic. So comfortably delicious.

She flipped the page again and stared at the employment ads. Suddenly, her life was full of new options.

EIGHT

"I'm sorry, Ms. Neill," the cooly controlled voice said on the other end of the line. "Kyle Adams is out of the office right now. He did leave a message for you, though."

Hilary's eyebrows rose at that. "Yes?"

"You are to phone him this evening at seven."

"Home or office?" She hid the bristling irritation kindled by Kyle's order. She'd been here a week and a half and still hadn't gotten the man on the phone, although she'd left numerous messages. Her anger flared, fueled by months of vague doubts that had eroded her feelings for a fiancé who always put business first.

"He didn't say, though probably he'll still be at the office," the receptionist answered.

"Thank you." Hilary barely resisted slamming the receiver into the cradle. Instead, she rubbed her forehead and considered whether to leave a succinct message on his home answering machine. No, it wasn't fair to blame Kyle for being exactly what she'd once wanted. Was it his fault she'd changed her mind?

Maybe, if he'd taken more time off from work, if he'd even once let his passion for her push him into doing something silly and romantic, something decidedly unbusinesslike . . .

She dialed another number on the old-fashioned rotary dial phone. A familiar voice answered.

"I'm glad it's you," Hilary said. "I need to ask a favor."

At seven o'clock, Hilary started to phone Kyle, then cradled the receiver. She'd called later after Sam left. For that matter, if Kyle was near a phone, he could call, too. Let him pay for the call this time.

Even so, a cloud hovered over the entire evening as she waited for the phone to ring. Sam seemed to sense her tension and he kept the conversation light. Not once did he touch her. She was beginning to think she'd imagined that toe-curling kiss and that magical interlude in the moonlight.

She did get around to phoning Kyle but not until after ten. She got the answering machine, both at the office and at his apartment. They played telephone tag for the next four days, thanks to the network of answering machines, including the discreet black model she'd installed in Ben's upstairs office.

She was tapping away at the rented typewriter when the office phone rang late Thursday. She hesitated, letting it ring three times in case it was a response to one of the resumé packages she'd mailed earlier in the week. It wouldn't do to appear too desperate.

She needn't have worried. Kyle's smooth greeting was businesslike, but warmer than she'd remembered. Perhaps the warmth had always been there, but she'd missed it.

"Glad I finally caught you, dear," he said.

Her stomach lurched with apprehension. "We need to talk."

"Can it wait until tomorrow? I heard from the developer down there, the one I told you about. He wants to meet with us."

"Why? The housing development is out of the running."

"I just don't want you to rule anything out until you have all the facts in hand. Let's just listen to what the guy has to say."

Hilary sighed. She hadn't expected it would be this hard to even get to the subject *she* wanted to discuss.

"Kyle, I don't want to talk about the property now. We need to talk about *us*."

"I know, darling. We haven't had much time together lately. But tomorrow—"

"Kyle," she broke in. "This is important."

"Then why don't you tell me?" he suggested. "Just a second. Hold on." Voices intruded in the background, loud at first, and then muffled, as if Kyle had covered the receiver with his hand. After a moment he came back on the line.

"Hilary, we'll talk tomorrow. I promise. Right now I have a client here. 'Bye, dear." He clicked down the receiver before she had a chance to suggest she might not be home then. The Chandlers had invited her to a pig roast to celebrate a sixtieth wedding anniversary.

Imagine being married that long. Imagine caring enough to stay together more than half a century. She opened the desk drawer and pulled out the heavy ring she'd kept there since returning from Sam's house last Saturday. It no longer belonged on her finger, but she missed what it symbolized. And she was a little sad for the dreams that would be delayed a bit longer.

She set the ring back into the drawer, then hesitated. She ought to find a safer place for it. The wall safe would do if she could only find the combination among the box of paperwork the attorney had given her. Maybe Sam could help her find it when he returned from that conference in Denver. He might even know the combination.

She returned to work on the cover letter she'd been typing when Kyle called, but gave up after the third mistake in as many minutes. The letter could wait. She didn't need to find a job right away, though she didn't want to remain idle for long. This time, though, she could choose any job in any city she wanted. That was the nice part about being an heiress, even one of moderate proportions. She could afford to wait for the right job offer.

Friday dawned hot and humid, as usual. Hilary tried working on the employment listings she'd culled from other major newspapers at the main branch of the public library. But she couldn't work up much enthusiasm for the task. Perhaps she should take her time, decide where she wanted to live first. Without her ties to Kyle, her options would be wide open.

She headed for the attic again. Rummaging through her ancestors' belongings sounded like a lot more fun than applying for jobs she wasn't sure she wanted. By noon, she'd tried on two silk dresses that hadn't lost their luxurious feel, though they'd grown fragile with age. She left the attic door open so she could hear the phone, but to no avail. She wasn't surprised. She'd come to expect as much.

She wiped a bead of sweat from her forehead, then dried her hand on her cutoffs so she wouldn't stain the faded silk. If she stayed for any length of time, she'd buy an air conditioner, at the very least a window unit for the second-floor office. She couldn't understand how Great-Uncle Ben withstood the heat. Weren't the elderly supposed to be susceptible to heatstroke?

Maybe he'd had a summer cottage in Saskatchewan that nobody knew about. Maybe she'd sell the Chicago house and buy a summer cottage someplace cool, like north of the arctic circle. For now, though, she'd find another way to cope.

So, she did what any self-respecting, heat-driven career woman on a sabbatical does. She took a quick shower and went shopping.

Three hours in an air-conditioned mall did wonders for her sense of humor. It also added a couple of bargain blouses to her wardrobe and a pair of beanbag chairs for lounging in front of the television she'd bought. There were limits to the number of checkers games she'd play. She needed a little electronic entertainment. She craved it.

She was on her way to the parking lot when a display window caught her eye, two display windows, really. They flanked the entrance to a lingerie shop, part of a chain noted for its sexy, yet tasteful undergarments and nightwear. In one window, the headless mannequins modeled summer-bright teddies and short robes. In the opposite, an older woman in jeans adjusted a discreetly cut red robe on one mannequin. While Hilary watched, she gave the robe a couple of light pats, then proceeded to strip the other mannequin of a soft peach-and-ivory lace ensemble.

Sheer elegance, Hilary thought as she stepped into the shop, but probably out of her price range. Besides, she couldn't even use her honeymoon as an excuse for buying something that extravagant. She'd cancelled it. She just had to tell the groom.

"Could I help you?" The sales clerk's voice startled her out of her thoughts. She realized then that she'd been staring, that both the saleswoman and the window dresser watched her with knowing looks that already anticipated a sale.

She shook her head. "No, thanks. I'm just looking."

The saleswoman's smile widened. "Let me know if you'd like to try anything on."

Hilary hesitated, glancing around at the brightly draped display racks. "Do you have any more like the set she's taking out of the window?"

"Oh, the bridal display? The spring and summer lines are on the clearance racks, except for the peignoir set with the pearl beads at the neckline. Is that what you wanted to see?"

"I'm not getting married," she said, then wondered why she'd told a stranger that.

"Then are you looking for a gift or shopping for yourself? We just put some lovely new teddies out this morning."

Hilary smiled, more to herself than at the woman who was being so helpful, almost too helpful. It was an interesting thought, almost a novel one: shopping for herself in a lingerie store. She'd never been that frivolous before.

Perhaps it was time.

"The peach gown from the window display," she began. "Is it the only one you have? I'm not sure what size . . ." What sizes did nightwear come in? Small, medium, large or was the system like those confusing increments used for socks, underwear, and bras?

The woman frowned slightly. "Let me check, but I think that was the last one." She returned an instant later with the peach ensemble draped over her arm.

"Would you like to try it on?"

Hilary stared at the flowing silk, imagining the feel of it against her body. She didn't need it. She'd slept in her father's old T-shirts for years.

"I think I will try it on," she said, surprising herself.

Fifteen minutes later, she left the store, carrying one more package. Just the thought of it curled her toes. It wasn't as much an extravagance as it was a gift to herself. In buying it, she promised herself she wasn't throwing away her one chance at happiness, but by-passing an opportunity that wasn't quite right. She'd bought it to please herself. From now on, she'd be neither starry-eyed romantic nor hard-nosed pragmatist. She'd pay more attention to her instincts and her own feelings.

Lately, her feelings were very much directed at her enigmatic neighbor. She just wondered how reliable those feelings were. Her wild, impetuous side told her to simply enjoy them—and him—without worrying where it all would lead. But Kyle had been right about one thing—her impetuousness usually led her into difficulties.

She stopped twice on the drive home, once to get a drink and again at a roadside stand offering lush pots of summer flowers at bargain prices. Figuring they'd brighten the place up, she bought enough to fill the backseat.

Once she reached home, she gathered up the smaller packages and headed for the back door. Inside, she spied a torn sheet of paper on the floor, lying as if it had been slipped under the door.

Sorry I missed you. See you after I get back from town. It was signed with a scrawl that remotely resembled Sam's name. Hilary dropped her packages on the table and returned to the car for the beanbag chairs. She put them and the portable television in one of the spare rooms upstairs. Maybe she could coax Sam into watching a movie with her, she thought.

After a quick change into her cool summer shorts and cropped top, she played back the message on the answering machine. It was only a sales pitch on vinyl siding. She shuddered to think what Sam would say if she defiled Neill House with that stuff.

She debated what to do next, but nothing sounded too appealing. She ought to put away the rest of her packages. She ought to finish the job applications. Instead, she gathered up the gardening gloves she'd bought that morning and attacked the neglected flower beds in front of the house. She planted the lush petunias she'd been unable to resist buying from the roadside stand. Then she pinched back the half-grown fall mums that framed the front porch. Never mind that she might not be there to see them bloom. Well-tended landscaping helped sell houses, according to Kyle. Besides, the steady, rhythmic work loosened the tight knot of tension building in her neck. She still had to talk to him.

She was just tucking the last plant into a hole when Sam's battered sneakers appeared next to the trowel. Her eyes quickly lifted, taking in the ripped, disreputable jeans, the ragged T-shirt, and the chocolate eyes twinkling down at her.

"Looks like you're thinking of staying awhile," he said.

She shrugged, turning back to the flowers. "I got these cheap. I thought they might perk the place up, especially if I decide to sell."

He didn't answer, just bent to help her scoop dirt around the roots, then dragged the hose over to water the root ball.

"The yard is looking better," he finally said. She couldn't tell whether he was changing the subject or not, his expression was so vague.

"A little water and fertilizer never hurt anything green," she retorted, then stole a look at him. Did he really care whether she stayed? He'd made it obvious he didn't want her to sell the land, but that had nothing to do with her personally. His frown told her nothing. It could have been triggered as much by the spots on the nearby rose bushes as by her words.

"I found some rose dust in the shed, but I didn't find a sprayer," she said when he fingered a leaf.

"You can use mine," he said. "So, how about Mexican for supper tonight?"

She grinned. "My place or yours?"

He winked, shedding whatever had bothered him as a duck sheds water. "The tortillas are heating in my oven as we speak."

"I'll be over as soon as I finish here," she promised, her mood lightening. Why worry about his motives? Just enjoy the time. Enjoy him. *And be grateful that he made you realize Kyle wasn't the one for you.*

"Deal, and don't forget to close the barn door, either," Sam said, stepping backward toward the driveway.

Hilary glanced from him to the door in question. Wide enough for a dump truck to pass through, it opened onto the gaping hallway of the huge, almost empty building. "Can't have the dust or those old tools getting out, can we?" she retorted.

"It's part of taking care of a place like this," he said. "Closing doors, putting tools away, checking the fences." For him, it was the proper way of doing things.

"Why should I worry when I have you to do that for me?" she said.

He ignored her sarcasm. "Half an hour, no later. We'll play cutthroat to decide who does dishes."

"Get out your rubber gloves, Langford, or you're going to have dishpan hands," she called as he spun around and trotted toward home.

"You'll have to play better than last night," he tossed out over his shoulder.

She stuck her tongue out at his retreating back. A decidedly childish response, but she didn't care. He made her feel lighter, more free than she remembered feeling in months. There were no words big enough to describe it. She only knew that the high point of her day now centered on the smile he brought to her lips and the answering light she found in his eyes.

Hilary watched him until he rounded the curve and disappeared from sight. Then she stowed her tools in the little room at the front of the barn. She hurried to the house for a quick rummage in the attic for the book she'd found that morning, then a lightning fast shower and change of clothes.

She was at his door in twenty-seven minutes flat. Hot, spicy smells drifted through the screen and her stomach growled in response. She leaned on the bell, just as she'd done every other time this week when she'd waited on his porch.

"I'm coming, all right." His voice preceded the flopping tap of his footsteps. He must have changed from the sneakers to the even more disreputable thongs he'd worn the other night.

"No hurry," she assured him as he came into sight. "I just like the sound of those chimes. Didn't Edison invent the doorbell? No, that was certainly too late for this house. Perhaps it was Ben Franklin, a year or two after the kite incident."

"Really?" Sam looked down his nose at her, his professorial expression deepening the furrows of his brow. That look must have destroyed more than one freshman. Right now, though, a huge tomato squirt on his collar spoiled the effect. "Just a minute. I have something to show you," he added.

He picked up a box from the hall chest and handed it to her. "I want you to keep these. They belong in the family."

Hilary didn't have to open it to know what was inside. "The pearls?"

He nodded slowly, an anxious expression on his face.

She opened the box and smiled at the fragile strand lying against the faded scarlet lining. "They're beautiful. But they mean more to you than they do to me. I wouldn't feel right if I took them." She handed the box back to him, pressing it firmly into his hand. She laid the book she'd found on top of the box.

"You're making this difficult," he said.

She shrugged as she passed him on the way to the kitchen. "Only if you don't accept my decision," she said. "Now, to change the subject, I found that book in the attic. I thought you might want it, considering what you're doing out there." She gestured in the general direction of the garden.

"*Bruist's Family Kitchen Garden*," he said, thumbing to the title page. "Copyright 1847. Where did you find this?"

"In the bottom of a box of old household accounts. Since you're into the old-fashioned ways, I thought you might find it interesting."

He seemed surprised. "Been digging through the family papers, huh? I thought you didn't have time for that now."

"I was bored with typing cover letters yesterday, so I decided to go up there and prowl around. I think the search for the family photos whetted my curiosity."

"Find anything else interesting?"

"A couple of neat hats and a great flapper dress. One of the trunks had some old clothes, probably dating back to the nineteenth century, judging from the styles."

Sam nodded. "Ben used to bring them out once in awhile when they were giving a program for the volunteers at Missouri Town, kind of a mini-class in period clothes."

"I tried one of the dresses on," she admitted. "It was fun, though I was scared to death I'd rip it, especially in the waist. Whoever owned it must have had a tight corset. I can't imagine why you people actually wear that stuff. It's hot and uncomfortable."

"Come with me sometime and try it," he suggested.

Hilary laughed skeptically. "I don't think so. I'll leave that hobby to you," she said, then raised her eyes to his thoughtful ones. "Except it isn't just a hobby to you, is it?"

He handed her the book. "Read through this," he suggested. "Especially the parts about flowers. After a few pages you'll begin to understand why living history is so fascinating. It's not just names and dates in a textbook, it's about what real people used to do every day. You like flowers—think what it might be like to grow roses without fungicides and so on. Take organic gardening, for instance. It's not a new trend. It was the only thing these people had going.

She smiled. "You're on your soapbox again."

Sam scratched his head as a sheepish grin stole onto his lips. "Sorry. Occupational hazard."

She set the book on the table and picked up the knife to finish slicing the tomatoes on the drainboard.

"I'm cooking tonight," he reminded her, reaching for the knife.

"Then the cook's wearing dinner." She touched a finger to his collar. The now familiar heaviness settled in her midsection. She turned away before her expression could give her away. "Anyway, you should know better than to argue with a woman holding a knife," she continued, giving the tomatoes a hard chop for emphasis.

"Especially a woman with vicious tendencies," he agreed. "If you play the corporate game like you play cutthroat, you should be CEO in a couple of years."

Hilary tossed him a doubtful glance over her shoulder. "A couple of decades maybe, if I can stomach it that long. Besides, haven't you heard of the glass ceiling? Most women get stuck in middle management, if they make it that far.''

''Gee, a cynic at the age of . . . How old are you?''

''Old enough to face reality,'' she parried. ''I'm unemployed, remember?''

''That was your choice, wasn't it?''

''In retrospect, maybe not a good one. I have, however, come up with all sorts of euphemistic reasons for passing up a promotion and refusing a transfer.''

''Why don't you start your own accounting firm?''

She hesitated. ''I considered it. I don't think I'm ready yet—not enough experience. Not many would trust their financial health to a firm whose senior partner is under thirty.'' She dumped the chopped tomatoes into a bowl and set it on the table next to the guacamole and shredded lettuce.

''What are you going to do?'' He stared down at the spicy meat mixture he was stirring, his face a mask of mild indifference that warred with his tense stance. She got the feeling there were all sorts of coded messages hovering in the air between them. She couldn't decipher a single one.

She hesitated. ''I've applied for a few positions.''

''In Chicago?''

''All over. Chicago, Denver, San Antonio, Kansas City.''

Warmth softened his studied indifference. ''Then you haven't ruled out the possibility of moving here.''

''Not yet,'' she agreed. His interest chased away the inner chill. She wanted him to care what she did, whether she stayed or left, but she wasn't sure it should matter. That was the trouble with feelings, they didn't care about shoulds and shouldn'ts. She had to depend on her brain to remind her of side issues like being on the rebound and the polar differences between their goals and life-styles.

Sam would make a great friend, although she'd never had a friend affect her quite the way he did. Too bad she couldn't shake her solid Midwestern upbringing and have a fling with him. But that was no more likely than any lasting relationship between them. As partners, they didn't match up very well.

Or did they?

They'd fallen into an easy relationship, sharing dinner and dishes, talking for hours, teasing and taunting, or sharing long, comfortable silences. And then, there was Neill House. Sam loved it. She had been fascinated by it from the first moment she'd seen it seven years ago, but for different reasons originally. Nevertheless, she was becoming more and more interested in the history of the place and in her family's history, which were both so intimately entwined.

More importantly, Sam listened to her, really listened. Kyle, with whom she had so much in common, never centered his attention so directly on her, not for any length of time.

Hilary chewed on that for the next two hours, through the meal, the cleanup, and three straight losses at the checkerboard.

"You should turn pro," she suggested when his deadpan expression split into a grin after a particularly cunning move. He'd effectively trapped her remaining two pieces, leaving her the choice of forfeiting or sending her men on suicide missions, and she didn't even care. His warlock spell had completely destroyed her competitive spirit over the last few days.

"Can't make a living at checkers," Sam replied. "That's why I teach. There's always plenty of pliable young minds out there in need of marketable college degrees. Another game? I'll spot you two kings."

She scowled and began resetting the board. "Don't insult me. I'm just a little off tonight."

Sam grasped her hands in his own, curling her fingers around the checker pieces she was holding. "If you're not going to pay any more attention than that, let's put the game away."

Hilary focused her gaze on the board, then sighed. She'd mixed the reds and blacks. "Sorry, I was thinking about something else."

"Kyle?" Sam's eyes pinned her, probing for the truth. She couldn't quite give it to him so she fudged a little bit.

"I was thinking you weren't telling the whole truth just now." *It was only a little white lie, a slight shifting. She had been thinking of him, just not in this particular context.*

"About teaching?" He reached across the board, then halted, glancing up at her. "You're right. I used to have some crazy idea that I could make a difference, that I could influence all those young minds."

"I imagine most teachers feel that way at some point," Hilary said.

Sam shrugged and headed for the refrigerator. "Maybe at first," he continued, handing her a cola and getting another for himself. "Back then, I thought I could make them see that the past is the key to the future. And maybe they would someday make good citizens and good legislators because of it. Or maybe they'd call in an archeology team if they found an Indian burial ground in a field instead of planting corn on it."

"You're an idealist," she accused, leaning back in her chair.

He closed the refrigerator and leaned against the door. "Nope, but I don't believe anybody has the right to complain without offering something constructive.

This is my way of being constructive. It's a little hard to measure in terms of dollars, unless you count my unimpressive salary.''

He spoke with casual ease, but she sensed the strong beliefs underlying his words. "Money doesn't matter to you?''

"It buys food, paint, a few things like that.''

"You never wanted to be rich?'' she continued, pushing. She'd never met anyone who didn't harbor a little honest envy beneath his supposedly altruistic values. It was only human.

"If I were rich, I'd make you an offer on Neill House that you couldn't refuse. That way, we'd both get what we want.''

Hilary slowly shook her head. "I'm not sure what I want these days. I'm getting kind of attached to the place, knocking pipes and all.''

"So, stay.'' Deep sincerity hummed in his voice.

"Sometimes I want to very much,'' she whispered.

"Sometimes,'' he repeated solemnly. "It's a start.'' Moving with slow deliberation, he picked up the checkerboard and slid the pieces into the box, then stowed the game in the cabinet.

"You're not wearing your ring,'' he pointed out. It was the first time he'd mentioned it. "I haven't seen you wear it since—'' His eyes darkened with satisfaction and something less definable as his words trailed off.

"Have you told Kyle?'' he asked.

She popped the tab of the cola and stood, staring off into the falling dusk outside the window. She knew what he meant. The removal of her engagement ring held a symbolism he couldn't fail to miss. She wasn't ready to marry Kyle, not when her body responded so fervently to another man.

"I've had about thirty seconds on the phone with

him. I need to go to Chicago soon, anyway. I'll tell him then. It's better that way than over the phone. In the meantime, I'm going to hang onto Neill House and see if I can come up with a way for it to be self-supporting.''

"You won't manage it by giving tours,'' Sam said with a humorless laugh. "That's been tried in this area before. It took a dying millionaire's trust fund to save the place.''

"I was thinking of a bed and breakfast or offices.''

Sam looked skeptical. "I'd hate to see that happen, but I'm not blind to reality. It beats the gas station idea.''

"That wasn't mine,'' Hilary reminded him. "And now, I'd better get going. I need to call my mother tonight. I don't want to call too late because she has to get up early in the morning.''

"You could call from here.''

"I don't think so,'' she said. "Not on your bill.''

He nodded. "Then I'll walk you back.''

"You don't have to. I've gotten used to the night noises.''

He took her hand and raised it to his lips. "A gentleman always walks the lady to her door, and then he wishes her good night in an appropriate manner.'' He kissed her open palm lightly. Her knees turned to butter.

"Always?''

"Always,'' he repeated. "For Mrs. Chandler and the other ladies of the park, there's this.'' He planted a chaste kiss on her cheek. "For their granddaughters, there's this.'' Another kiss, this time placed lightly on her brow.

"Which do I rate?'' A loaded question, but suddenly she felt like playing with dynamite. Anything to burst the breathless tension bubbling through her.

His lips touched her brow again. Before disappointment could register, his touch edged toward her hairline, then traced a trail of heat to the base of her neck. Her eyelids drooped closed. He kissed them, too, and her nose, then a path around her mouth. When he finally reached her mouth, she was practically limp from wanting him.

She leaned closer, wrapping her arms around his neck. Her lips met his boldly, giving as much as she took. He lifted his head slowly, his eyes radiating more warmth than she'd ever imagined, and something else as well. Tenderness, triumph, and desire, all tangled into one in the even planes of his face and behind his warlock dark eyes.

"All that, huh?" she whispered. He touched her lips briefly, before releasing her, though his fingers still clung to her hand. He tugged her toward the door.

"Let's go call your mother," he said.

He made it onto the porch before he released a wild, eerie yell that made the hair on the back of her neck stand on end.

"What are you doing?" She squealed when he tugged her off the porch and twirled her around.

"That, love, was a rebel yell," he said, depositing her back on the ground. "It's the local version of the cave-man chest pounding."

Hilary groaned. "Great. Now the entire countryside knows about it." Still, she kept her hand in his. It felt good there. She felt good, too, too good. She'd never be able to call her mother tonight.

It took longer than usual to make the brief walk between the two houses because they lingered at the gate, fiddling with the sagging hinge. Then they picked orange daylilies in the dark. It wasn't until they were nearly around the corner of the house that she remembered the barn door. She couldn't remember shutting it.

Still rattling on about the possibilities for the flower beds, she stole a glance at the barn, hoping he wouldn't notice. But the wide door was closed. Odd, but then she'd been so distracted earlier she could have slogged through knee-deep mud without knowing it.

Hilary climbed the stairs and turned the knob. She started inside, but Sam hesitated. The light shining from the kitchen window revealed his uncertain expression. "I'll see you tomorrow," he said, handing her the blossoms he'd picked.

"You aren't coming in?" Disappointment seared through her. She didn't want the evening to end.

"Do you want me to?" His husky tone warned that he was asking for more than permission to cross the threshold. It was time for honesty.

"I'm not sure about a lot of things, but this I know," she said, "I want you to come inside and help me find a vase for these. I want you to wait while I call Mom. Then, I wouldn't mind digging through boxes all night or talking or whatever you want to do. I suddenly find that I don't want to say good-bye." Not suddenly, she knew, but that was too much to admit.

He squeezed her hand. "You're still an engaged woman."

"Technically," she said with a scowl as she remembered the frustratingly brief conversation with Kyle the day before. Maybe she should try calling him again.

"By the way, do you know the combination to the wall safe in Ben's office? I need to use it."

"That I can help you with," he said. "I'll show you where Ben hid the combination."

He followed her inside, his hands resting easily on her shoulders. "A vase first," he said, steering her toward the dining room after she'd deposited the blooms on the counter. "I'll trim the stems."

"In the sideboard, bottom right," Hilary said. "I found them the other day. Goodness, I can't believe I left these lights on."

She rounded the corner and gasped, stopping so abruptly she stumbled. She righted herself immediately, grabbing the solid door frame. She felt as if all the blood had drained from her body. The packages she'd left carelessly stacked on the dining room table were scattered, some opened, some seemingly undisturbed. But it was the man seated across the room who drew her eyes.

Smiling appreciatively, Kyle held the peach satin-and-lace gown at arm's length. Hilary wanted to turn and run, but he caught sight of her before she could make her frozen limbs move.

"Hilary, dear," he exclaimed, rising from his seat. "Are you saving this for the honeymoon, or would you consider modeling it a little sooner?"

NINE

Hilary's mouth moved, but no sound came out. She took a step backward and bumped into Sam's solid frame. His steadying hand settled on her shoulder.

"I guess you won't be calling your mother now," he said.

"I guess not." Her voice was whisper thin, but functioning again. She cleared her throat and stepped into the room, away from his support. Might as well face the music. It would be easier, though, if Kyle weren't waving that nightgown around like a flag on Veteran's Day.

"Why didn't you let me know you were coming? I would have been here," she said, her voice growing stronger with each word. She sounded like any loving fiancée and felt like a cheap fraud. She stole an uncomfortable glance over her shoulder at Sam. He leaned against the fine-grained trim that outlined the doorway as if he belonged there. His eyes held a challenge and a glitter of something else she couldn't quite place.

"Did you fly?" she continued, turning back to Kyle. There was no car in the yard, so he must have.

Kyle nodded. "I thought I'd surprise you," he said. "I wasn't sure until the last minute that I'd make it."

A low whistle sailed out from behind her. "Must have been quite a taxi fare from the airport," Sam interjected. "What is it, fifty, sixty miles from here?"

"Oh, I'd thought you'd left," Kyle said dismissively, then smiled at Hilary. "I put the rental car in the barn. Hilary, dear, you really should be more careful. It's not like you to leave doors standing wide open for anyone to walk in and make off with whatever they want."

She couldn't think how to answer, because it was exactly like her to do that sort of absentminded thing lately. She'd gotten a bit lax without the frequent reminders of police sirens. Fresh air and the occasional fox didn't seem to be very threatening.

Kyle carelessly dropped the gown over the back of the chair and wrapped his arms around her. "I've missed you, my dear," he said, squeezing her against him.

Except for the cold knot in her stomach, the embrace was like any other in the two years she'd known him. But the crack of emotion in his voice caught her by surprise. It twisted the knife in her chest. Her arms circled his waist, reluctantly returning the hug. Over his shoulder, she watched the peach silk flutter down across the chair seat, covering the intricate stitches Sarah's needle had worked years ago. The movement seemed symbolic of the tangled web she'd allowed to trap her.

"Kyle, what are you doing here?" She pulled away, glancing self-consciously over her shoulder at Sam. Except for the faint tightening of his jaw, he hadn't moved.

"Yes," Sam agreed. "You really should have called. Hilary could have warned you about the hot water situation."

"I beg your pardon?" Kyle stared at Sam as if he wasn't quite operating on all six cylinders.

"He means the propane leak," she explained. "The plumber's still repairing the line between the tank and the house. I haven't had hot water or a working stove for about a week now."

"Week and a half," Sam corrected.

"You *have* been roughing it, dear."

Hilary released a dry laugh. "I've managed." Actually, she'd jogged over to Sam's for her showers, but she didn't think that answer would go over well.

"She does this trick with garden hoses," Sam said.

Hilary squinted at him, then felt herself blanch. How did he know about *that*? Had she forgotten to put the hoses away? At the moment, she couldn't remember yesterday, let alone the details of a one-time experiment more than a month ago.

Kyle looked skeptical. "Garden hoses? Sounds kinky."

Sam smiled. "Interesting pun. But no, she just lays them in the sun to heat up during the day, then showers after the sun goes down and she's made sure nobody else is around. I'm really not sure what she does about the mosquito problem. They can be a terrible nuisance around here."

"This was your idea?" Kyle's expression grew cold. He didn't even look at her but fixed his gaze on Sam. A chill ran down her spine, more for herself than for Sam's sake since her own feelings were approaching red-hot fury.

"No, sir," Sam said in his low drawl. "Your *fiancée* is pretty clever. She puts a sign on the gate, 'Guard dog, honk please.' I never believed the dog part, though I didn't bother her when the sign was up, either. After she knocked me down the stairs, I've done my best not to make her *really* mad."

Hilary could have cheerfully strangled the man—no, men, both of them. As it was, she could feel her blood pressure rising with each outrageous word. *But how had he known?*

The thoughts flashed through her mind with lightning speed. She hadn't left the clues lying around. She definitely remembered taking down the sign and putting away the hoses at dawn the day after the outdoor shower. He hadn't been at the blasted church supper that night. He'd been spying on her. She flushed crimson at the realization.

"Is he kidding?" Kyle asked, dropping an arm across her shoulder. The spark of interest in his eyes and the intimate way he pressed against her boded trouble. She couldn't decide whether he was staking out his territory for Sam's benefit or was simply turned on by the idea of an after-dark shower outdoors.

She hadn't done the garden hose thing once this trip, but admitting it would only make matters worse. Somehow, she didn't think Kyle would react well to the knowledge that she frequently popped over to the "weird caretaker's house" for dinner and a shower. He was bound to ask what else had happened. She didn't want to end their relationship on that note. There were ways to tell and ways not to.

"Kyle and I need to talk," she said, with a pointed look at Sam.

He jerked upright, seemingly startled by his own rudeness. "Oh, of course. I'm sorry. Nice seeing you again, Kyle." He lifted his hand in a light wave, though his eyes were anything but casual as they met hers. Warlock-dark, they dared her to think of what might have happened tonight had Kyle not appeared.

She didn't want to think of it, not as she stood next to the man she'd promised to marry and listened to the departing footsteps of the man she wanted. The footsteps stopped, then retraced the pathway to the dining room.

"In all the excitement, I'll bet you forgot about calling your mother," Sam reminded her.

"Thanks. I had forgotten."

"Why not do it before you get distracted?" he suggested. "I just thought of something I need to ask the real estate expert."

"I beg your pardon?" Hilary said. He wasn't leaving. What was he up to now?

"It's about that developer you mentioned. I wonder if he's the same guy who approached Ben about a year ago."

"Really?" Kyle's arms dropped away from her. "Was it Lyle Briggs by any chance?"

Sam looked worried. "That's him. He has a reputation around here. He's running just a few steps ahead of a grand jury, if you know what I mean."

"Why didn't you tell me before?" Hilary interjected. Sam's expression was a shade too worried, too earnest.

Kyle's attitude changed from polite dismissal to wary interest. Sam had punched the right buttons to turn Kyle's professional instincts on full force. She suspected he was playing Kyle along again. When he winked, she knew.

She flashed a murderous look at Sam. A wiser man would have backed away from her anger. Sam only winked again. She bit her lip, tasting blood.

"Do you have to go just yet?" Kyle asked. "Perhaps we should hear this, don't you think so, dear?"

"I'm going to call my mother now," she said, ducking out from under Kyle's arm. "And I'm going to pretend this conversation never happened." *Until I get you alone,* she added silently as she raked Sam with her eyes. For an instant, he looked shaken, then the shutters maddeningly covered his thoughts as they had so many other times.

"Fine," he said with a dismissive nod. "Suppose we compare notes? Maybe we can save the grand jury a little time and money." Sam finally left the doorway and opened the cabinet where Uncle Ben's Scotch stock was stored. "It's not that I'm against development, though there are some folks around here who don't want anything to change. I'd hate to see someone of Briggs's ilk get a foothold, though."

"I give up," she muttered, throwing her hands up in frustration. Neither man paid any attention to her, focusing warily on each other instead. Maybe they'd strangle one another while she was upstairs. That would save her the trouble. Failing that, she could always kick them both out of her house.

But she wouldn't. Even with her blood pounding angrily in her ears, she knew that wasn't the answer. She didn't want to hurt Kyle, but she had to. And she didn't want to lose Sam, though she wasn't sure she actually had him.

She halted on the landing, tapping her chipped nails restlessly against the cabbage rose wallpaper. She didn't know what to make of the recent turn of events. Her anger eased as she considered the possible reasons behind Sam's behavior—nosiness, dislike, or perhaps even jealousy.

"Actually, everything is an even bigger mess," she told her mother a few minutes later. She shifted the phone to the other ear, cradling it against her shoulder while she decided what to tell and what to keep to herself. In the end, she settled on only the bare fact that she'd decided not to marry Kyle. The rest would work itself out in time.

"And how did he take that?"

"I haven't told him yet, though it's not for lack of

trying," she said. "You know how Kyle is. I may have to tie him into a chair to get his undivided attention." At the moment the idea had its merits, she decided with a quiet chuckle. Maybe she should add a gag, no, two gags and an extra chair for Sam.

"That's funny?" Her mother's puzzled voice interrupted her revengeful thoughts.

"Think about it, Mother."

"You're right." Quiet amusement mingled with the concern in her mother's voice. "Kyle would probably chant mortgage amortization tables under torture. Oh, Hilary, I was so afraid you'd marry him. You seemed so determined."

"We have a great deal in common," she reminded her mother. "It wouldn't have been a bad marriage." A comfortable one, but lonely in ways she'd just begun to realize, she added silently. Two careers, two incomes, two hard-nosed professionals doing their best for capitalism. She wasn't very proud of herself.

"You would never have come first with Kyle," her mother said seriously. "Just like he wouldn't have been first with you. In marriage, you should be first with one another or it isn't worth the trouble."

Hilary was silent for a moment. It was so simple. "You would have saved me a lot of trouble by saying that sooner."

"Would you have listened?"

"Probably not," Hilary admitted. "But you would have had the chance to say I told you so."

"I'll tell your father in the morning. He still thinks Kyle is a perfect match for you, more fool him. He always takes everyone at face value, never looks any deeper."

Hilary laughed at the gentle disdain in the older woman's voice. If anyone else had said that about the man, she would have clobbered them with her big marble rolling pin.

"Mom, I'm not sure yet how to tell—" Footsteps on the stairs cut her short. "Never mind, someone's coming. I'll call in a few days."

She'd just cradled the receiver when Sam peered into the room. "Finished with your call?"

"Just now." Hilary rose from her chair. "Where's Kyle?"

"Putting his suitcase in the green room."

At least he hadn't headed straight for hers, though that was due more to Sam's presence than any sensitivity on Kyle's part. Kyle had an old-fashioned sense of propriety, at least where his image with the outside world was concerned.

"Fine," she said, wincing as she paced across the room and back. She felt a twinge of regret and even resentment that Kyle had finally decided to put her ahead of business. Why couldn't he have used the telephone like any other time?

"You'll tell him?" Sam sounded edgy.

"Of course, but I can't very well do it with you here."

"Maybe I should be here, in case—"

"In case what? Kyle isn't violent, for heaven's sake. I may have been mistaken about him, but I'm not a complete fool," she said, speaking in a low hiss. She shot Sam a warning look when Kyle's footsteps sounded in the hall.

Sam looked grim. "You said something about the wall safe?"

She glanced beyond him into the hallway where Kyle had appeared. Sam stepped aside to let the taller man into the room.

"It can wait. I won't need it after all."

Sam looked puzzled, then shrugged. "Whatever.

Since I'm here, though, I'll go ahead and show you where Ben hid the combination.''

"There wasn't anything in the papers from the attorney?'' Kyle asked as he settled onto a corner of the desk near Hilary.

"I didn't see it. I suppose I should have asked, but I didn't think to at the time,'' she replied. She stepped aside as Sam reached for the center drawer of the desk. She remembered too late what she'd left in the small compartment at the front.

"Why is your engagement ring there?'' Kyle asked, plucking it out as Sam pulled the drawer completely free of the slides. Hilary stared wide-eyed at Sam, pleading for his silence.

"Gardening,'' she improvised quickly. She wouldn't humiliate Kyle in front of Sam. She owed him more than that. "I took it off while I was working in the flower beds. Didn't you see the petunias by the front porch?''

"It was nearly dark when I got here,'' he said, staring down at the ring. The stone caught the light and sparkled brilliantly as it wobbled in his grasp. "Here, you'd better put it back on before you forget where you put it.''

The ring felt cold in her hand, not warm as it should have been from Kyle's hold. Or maybe the coldness was inside of her. She curled her finger around the ring, glancing surreptitiously at Sam. He caught her silent plea.

"About the combination,'' he began, lifting the drawer to eye level. "It's written along the edge here. It's in pencil so it might be a little hard to read.''

Kyle squinted in that direction, then leaned closer. "Is that a three or a five?''

She drew a deep, relieved breath. The confrontation

had been postponed for a more private moment. "I think it's a five," she confirmed. "I'll try it."

She didn't realize her hands were shaking until she started turning the safe dial. She jittered past the final number on her first attempt and had to start over. On her second try, the tumblers clicked into place, and the door swung open easily to reveal the barren steel cavity.

"No hidden treasure," Kyle commented, laying a hand lightly on her shoulder. "Disappointed?"

"I have quite enough already," she replied.

Sam cleared his throat. "I'd best be going. Sorry about the mess," he said, indicating the desk drawer balanced atop the file cabinet. She knew from his expresssion that wasn't what he meant, though. She clenched her fist tighter, feeling the stone and its metal setting cut into her flesh.

"It's really my mess. I'll take care of it," she said. "Thanks for your help."

He still hesitated. "Don't forget the plumber is coming early tomorrow to finish up," he said.

Kyle groaned behind her. "I was counting on sleeping in."

Sam looked from Hilary to Kyle, who now stood close enough for her to feel the heat of his body. "Not likely after he starts up the backhoe. I suppose you could always cancel."

Her eyes narrowed suspiciously. She got the distinct impression it wasn't the plumber Sam was concerned about.

"And be forced to do the garden-hose routine another night?" she said. "I'd rather not."

"No, thanks," Kyle agreed.

Sam shrugged. "There're always cold showers." His stiff posture told her he didn't care for the idea of her and Kyle and showers in juxtaposition. Kyle did, though. His hand slid suggestively up her back.

She felt smothered there in the doorway, caught between the two men. "I'll walk you out," she offered, edging toward the stairs. She'd clobber him over the head with the newel post and drag him out if that's what it took to give her time alone with Kyle to break the engagement. Sam must have misread her eagerness for him to leave because the concern faded from his eyes. He was suddenly in a hurry to go.

"The three of us have already done the staircase routine," Sam said sarcastically, moving on ahead of her. "I'm not too wild about the way it turned out last time, so I'd rather not repeat it, if you don't mind."

She halted. His tone stung more than the words themselves. She'd walked a shaky tightrope since she'd found Kyle holding the nightgown a little while ago. She got the distinct impression she'd just fallen off.

"Fine," she ground out, turning away.

"Hilary?" He waited until she faced him again before continuing. "Do you want me to turn off the lights and lock up on my way out? Save you and your *fiancé* the trouble." He hesitated at the foot of the stairs, his lips twisting into a smile that was anything but pleasant.

"Good night, Sam" was all she said. She turned and forced herself to walk back into the office.

Kyle was sliding the drawer into place. He pushed it closed and tested it a couple of times. Then he leaned back in the desk chair and propped his feet on the desk as if he owned it. "You didn't take the ring off to garden, did you?"

Dismay filled her. He knew.

She uncurled her palm and stared into the heart of the brilliant stone. "No." She sat down on the bare wood of the desktop. "It's time I returned your ring."

He looked pale, but resigned. "When you didn't come home for so long, and then when you didn't call right at seven the other night, I suspected as much. I just didn't realize how unsettling all these changes were to you. Sometimes I can be too focused on my work. I guess that's been the case lately."

Hilary watched him carefully. Something wasn't quite right. Where were the anger, the recriminations, the insulting accusations she'd steeled herself to withstand?

"I've thought about this a lot. Since I've been here, a lot of things about my life have become clear to me. And I'm not sure I like what I see."

Kyle sighed. "That's understandable under the circumstances. But I didn't expect unemployment to affect you so deeply, not when you have your inheritance to cushion you."

"You think this is just depression over a lost job?" Amazement overrode her dismay. He hadn't a clue to the truth.

"What else could it be?" He rose from his chair and wrapped her in an embrace that was probably meant to be comforting. "Come back to Chicago with me on Monday."

"Monday?" She hadn't thought beyond the next few minutes. He was planning to stay until Monday.

"Of course," then he groaned. "Sorry, I forgot about your car. I could cancel my flight and ride with you. If we left in the morning, we could make a leisurely drive of it. Talk, spend some much needed time together."

"That won't solve anything," she said firmly.

"Once you get settled into a new job you'll be back to normal," he continued. "Until then, don't worry about the wedding. I don't want to put any more pressure on you."

She pulled free and scooped up the ring from the desk. "I'm not going anywhere for awhile. You're welcome to stay here until your flight, but I think you'd better put the ring someplace safe, someplace where you won't forget to pack it.'' She turned and left the room without a backward glance. She didn't need one. His stunned look was permanently imprinted in her brain. He'd finally recognized how large the gap between them had grown.

It took her only a few minutes to tidy up downstairs and lock the doors. She gathered up her shopping bags and hauled them dispiritedly up the stairs. Damn Kyle and his blindness, anyway. He'd stolen the warm-spirited hope she'd felt when she'd carried the bags inside earlier. She shoved them into her closet, then hesitated. She'd left the gown on the chair.

She stomped back downstairs, hunting for the peach gown. It was nowhere to be found.

TEN

Hilary leaned against one of the tooled columns of the front porch, letting the breeze chase her uneasiness away. There was peace in the darkness, with the moon a hazy half circle behind a thin cloud cover. Clouds, but no rain. The ever-present heat and humidity reigned while the grass browned and the ground spawned wide cracks, which had swallowed her high heels the other day when she was silly enough to cut across the lawn to sniff the nicotiana. The air felt heavy and the night creatures were mostly silent. Even the mosquitoes seemed to have forgotten her existence. She wondered if that was a sign of rain.

Gentle raindrops to soak the earth, cool the air, beat a gentle tat-a-tat on the roof to lull her to sleep. What a wonderful thought. Tonight, though, there was no rest for her. Her eyelids felt like scratchy lead blankets. Yet, every time they drooped closed, her restless thoughts sent another surge of adrenalin through her system.

She scanned the shadows at the fringe of the yard, seeing only the muted edges and odd shapes the darkness made. Something moved down by the gate, probably a rabbit, or a raccoon, hardly worth noticing when her thoughts were so scary. It wasn't Halloween-type fear, or the kind a close call on the highway brings. This was deeper, shifting her self-concept on its axis.

She'd been so stupid. She shouldn't have run away to this house *to think*. Thinking wasn't what she'd needed. She'd known months ago she shouldn't marry Kyle, maybe not consciously, but she'd known. If she'd wanted to marry him, nothing would have stopped her from setting the date, and as soon as humanly possible. She was the impetuous one, right? If she'd wanted to marry Kyle, she wouldn't have been susceptible to Sam's kisses, to the fire in his fingertips, or the sweet seduction in his eyes.

But she'd let all the other changes in her life distract her from the truth. First, her judgment had been clouded by grief and the allegorical shifting sands beneath her feet. Then, she'd run blithely into the arms of a man she barely knew without saying good-bye to the one she'd promised herself to.

Excuses. No, she corrected herself, just reasons. She couldn't blame herself for being human and latching onto the one constant at her fingertips. Because of her blindness, she'd let Kyle go on believing she loved him, that she'd marry him. She suspected she hadn't managed to convince him otherwise last night. He'd gone to his room too quietly, with too little protest, almost as if he were humoring her. Calm acceptance wasn't in his character.

She frowned and leaned back, propping her foot against the opposite post. And what about Sam? He'd left in a fit of temper, probably thinking she'd been amusing herself with him and would now take up where she'd left off with her fiancé. Ex-fiancé, only he hadn't accepted the idea yet.

The half-moon shone through a break in the clouds, almost as brightly as it had that night the week before. The memory made her glance toward Sam's house, though she couldn't see it through the trees at the bend in the road. It didn't matter. In the moonlight, the odd shadow by the gate became a fencepost with a man perched atop it.

Sam.

He stared up at the house, at her. She couldn't see his eyes, yet she could feel them on her, raising goose-flesh and calling her to join him. He'd been there all along, she knew, watching over her. Even in anger, he'd thought it necessary to protect her, to be on hand for her call. Did he think Kyle would get violent over her rejection? She tried to be angry at Sam for that, for lacking faith in her judgment, but she utterly failed.

Still, she couldn't go to him, not yet, not with her mind so tired and muddled. She had things to settle first. Slowly, with soul-deep regret, she let herself back into the house. She didn't bother to lock the door, though. It wasn't necessary when she had her own personal sentinel. And what if the sentinel wanted to come in? She smiled at that thought as she climbed the stairs and slipped between the sheets.

She must have fallen asleep immediately, because she didn't remember anything past the instant her head touched the pillow. Even her dreams were uneventful, or at least unmemorable. She awoke slightly more clearheaded than usual, despite her late night. She even remembered to slip on a robe before venturing outside her room in search of eye-opening caffeine. There was no sense in giving Kyle the idea that she'd changed her mind and might once again welcome his attentions.

She needn't have bothered. The house appeared empty. Perhaps he'd gone home. The thought did more for her than three cups of strong coffee. She glanced out the window. The huge barn door gaped open, sunlight shining into the barren aisle where Kyle said he'd parked the rental car the night before. She couldn't believe her luck.

She raced up the stairs to the green room and tentatively pushed the door open. Spread open on the tangled bedcovers lay Kyle's leather garment bag, with yesterday's suit on top. The travel alarm clock she'd given him last Christmas was propped open on the bedside table. The digital face read 10:45. She'd slept through the roar of the plumber's backhoe. No, that wasn't possible. He hadn't shown up, or Kyle had interfered again and cancelled the work scheduled for this morning.

"Damn!" She stamped hard, forgetting she stood on bare, polished wood instead of shock-absorbing carpet.

She slid down the doorway, clutching her sore heel. Damn, he was still here. Damn, she'd slept so late. And damn, especially, the fact that she had to face all this without the benefit of a refreshing *warm* shower.

She stuck her head under the mound of pillows on her bed. Since that wouldn't solve anything, she did the sensible thing and got dressed instead. Faded cutoffs and an oversized mustard T-shirt made her slightly more presentable, though not much. Her hair twirled into cowlicks that might have been cute on a five-year-old. Dark circles and faint lines of strain showed beneath her eyes. Evidently, she hadn't slept as well as she thought. Maybe she'd scare Kyle away.

The sound of tires crunching in the gravel driveway brought her sharply alert. Since it wasn't the chugging thump of the plumber's truck or the roar of the backhoe, she knew it had to be Kyle returning from wherever he'd gone while she still slept. She stared in the mirror, consciously firming her resolve. She'd made her decision, and last night only underlined it as the correct one. Yet, the eyes staring back at her in the mirror were full of apprehension. She hated confrontations.

"Hey, Hilary! You up there?" Sam's voice startled her, jolting the apprehension into pleased surprise. She dropped the comb and hurried to the stairs.

He leaned casually against the newel post. He looked terrible, yet she could have kissed him she was so glad to see him. He didn't look as if he wanted to kiss her, though.

The effects of a night on a fencepost showed plainly on his tired face. When he straightened, he moved with a stiffness that made her want to knead the aches away for him. She curled her fingers around the banister, stroking the polished grain instead. His eyes didn't miss the movement.

"What are you doing here?" she asked. "Where's Kyle?"

"He's parking the car back in the barn. He borrowed my shower. It seems the man can't shave without hot water. And, no, I didn't set him straight about the garden-hose story," he added at her stern look.

"I returned the ring."

Relief flickered across his features, followed by a frown. "Why is he still here?"

That bothered her, too. "I'm not sure he's convinced I really mean it. He thinks it's just a stress reaction."

"Is it?"

"What do you think?"

He slowly shook his head. "You aren't the type. I do wonder, though, whether I'm just a summer romance for you."

She released a short, mirthless laugh. "I'm not sure what I am to you, professor. And it's not something I want to discuss right now when Kyle could return at any moment. And by the way, I'd like to hear the rest of the garden-hose story,'' she muttered, her indignation rising anew.

Heat flared in his eyes like a lit match, bright fire fading to a slow, steady burn. ''Another time, when there's nobody around to hear,'' he promised.

''Not good enough.''

''Then hear this, lady. Everything about you has been completely surprising, completely bewitching, from the moment I met you,'' he said, his voice low and smooth. ''I knew you were trouble when I first saw you on the stairs. When I saw you naked in the moonlight, I knew what kind of trouble. I never know what's going to happen next, but I can't wait to find out.''

The door slammed on the back porch. Sam tilted his head in that direction, waiting. When Kyle didn't appear immediately in the doorway, Sam continued speaking in a low tone that barely carried up the stairs.

''I came over earlier to see if he still planned to meet with the developer,'' he said, changing the subject while she was still reeling from his last declaration. ''I figured we might as well see what the guy's up to in the neighborhood. I hear we're not the only ones he's approached.''

Hilary frowned. ''I wasn't aware that I had been approached.'' She hurried down the stairs, pausing an impersonal distance from Sam. The refrigerator door opened, then slammed shut, and a chair creaked.

''That's Kyle?''

Sam smiled. ''He seemed sort of subdued this morning. Should I take that as a good sign?''

She hesitated. ''I do have the reputation of being a bear before I've had my coffee. Kyle isn't a complete fool.''

''Doesn't whistle in the morning, huh?''

She smiled. ''Does it really matter? About the developer . . .'' she prompted.

"According to Kyle," Sam said in a neutral tone, "the attorney for the estate passed the offer along to him quite awhile ago. Since you hadn't made up your mind and didn't want to talk about it, Kyle never mentioned the specifics."

Sam studied her as he spoke. She felt as if she were being examined under a microscope, and it wasn't her clothing or the condition of her skin in question. He wanted to know whether she'd been straight with him and if Kyle had told the truth. Kyle might omit a few facts, but she'd never known him to lie.

She shrugged. "He kept pushing about the plat, stuff like that. But, no, he never mentioned Briggs by name or even a developer in general until this week."

That seemed to satisfy Sam. "Briggs is coming out later today to talk to you."

She raised her brows. "Should I change clothes?"

His gaze lingered on her legs, then drifted upward. "Only if you're interested in doing business with the man."

"I'm not."

"Does this mean you've decided not to sell off the land?" Hope glimmered in his dark eyes.

"I don't want to, Sam. I probably won't have to, either."

He nodded, turning away. "In that case, I'll get you some coffee. You look like you didn't sleep well."

She aimed a playful jab at his shoulder. "Gee, thanks. You look pretty perky yourself," she said sarcastically. Reaching the kitchen, she took the cup he offered and settled into a chair at the far end of the scarred oak trestle table from Kyle.

Kyle looked up from the papers he was studying. "I saved you some doughnuts—chocolate-cream filled. They're in the refrigerator."

Hilary took a sip of coffee. Her stomach roiled from nerves. "I'll wait for lunch."

Kyle only nodded, his attention already buried in the newspaper. She ought to be angry, but her relief was too overwhelming. He was back to his usual all-business self. There was no sign of the jilted lover in him this morning. He'd always had the irritating ability to separate Kyle the man from Kyle the real estate agent. Her frown deepened. Today, he was the agent, and she didn't need his services in that area, either. She ought to tell him to bug off, go home, and never darken her door again. But that wasn't how she felt. She cared, just not enough and not in the right way.

The glimmer of an idea took form. By the time she started on her second cup of coffee, the idea had become a plan.

"Kyle, I've been thinking about the house. I want to open a restaurant here," she said.

Kyle simply stared. Sam choked, then sputtered. "A what?" he finally managed.

Somehow, she managed to keep her expression blandly sincere. "It's the most logical thing I could do," she said. "After all, I practically grew up in one."

"It's a little difficult to run a restaurant long-distance," Kyle said. "You'd have to relocate."

She nodded slowly. "I've considered that. This house is huge, plenty of space for the restaurant down here and an apartment for me in the attic. I'd have to renovate, although not as much as you'd think. Take this kitchen, for instance. It's plenty big enough to accommodate a commercial dishwasher, a Garland range, a couple of reach-in refrigerators, and so on. And knock down the wall between the parlor and dining room—"

"It's a load-bearing wall," Sam bellowed, finally coming out of his state of shock. She'd expected a reaction from him, but not quite this strong. He'd forgive her, though. Eventually.

"It is? Well, you'd know," she replied, frowning briefly while she chewed a knuckle. "That does present a problem. Of course, I suppose smaller dining areas would add to the atmosphere. There's this place in Pennsylvania, called Castle something or other. It used to be a mansion. The family fell on hard times and converted it into a high-class restaurant."

"Hard times wouldn't exactly describe your situation," Kyle reminded her.

"Of course not, at least not yet. And if I invest in my own business and run it with one eye on the bottom line and the other on the oven door, I should be able to turn a good profit. I'd bet that Castle place seats over five hundred. I wonder how many the fire department would certify Neill House for?"

Kyle folded his newspaper, carefully creasing it as he considered. Hilary grinned inwardly, recognizing the gesture.

"This isn't exactly a high-traffic marketplace, Hilary." That was Kyle, ever the real estate agent no matter what happened to him personally.

"I'm not talking about a McDonald's," she said. "I want to open the kind of restaurant people are willing to drive out of their way for, something with style and atmosphere and the kind of food you can't get anywhere else. Maybe I'll capitalize on the historical restoration of the place."

Sam looked ready to pop a blood vessel just from the anger pumping furiously beneath his flushed skin.

"Don't you think so, Sam?" she added before he could speak. "You were just saying the other day that a restaurant would be a good complement for the development, along with the quick-stop on your property."

"I was?" He watched her closely.

"Yes, remember?" She kicked him under the table, then covered with a sincere smile. Damn, he was slow on the uptake. "It was after the gas leak, when you were telling me that I should take steps to preserve the house and maybe give the public access to it. A museum would be one way, but it would take an enormously large sum to endow it, more than I have at my disposal. But a commercial venture, with responsible management, would be a perfect solution."

Sam sat frozen, staring at her as if she'd lost her mind. His features shifted almost imperceptibly. He nodded. "Yes, yes, now I remember. You'll recall I warned you about going in too deeply before you were ready. It'll take your place a while to develop a following." He nudged her leg, tracing the length of her skin. She realized with a start that his bare toes caressed her skin. Good heavens, he'd slipped off his shoes to play footsies. And he'd wondered what *she* would do next.

"I suppose I could start with just a few dining rooms and a small staff," she said, her voice going slightly breathless as the toes edged over her knees and up her thigh. She shot him a warning look. The foot stopped, but didn't retreat.

"I could open up more space as I needed it or use the upstairs for banquet rooms."

Sam scratched his chin, looking thoughtful. Hilary hoped Kyle didn't see the playful glint in his eyes. "I have a better idea." Yes, he'd definitely caught on. She only hoped he didn't carry the ruse too far.

Kyle snorted, leaning back in his chair. "This I have to hear."

"A bed and breakfast." Sam beamed as if he'd just announced the onset of world peace. His toes wriggled across her knees and down her leg.

She grabbed her near-empty coffee cup and shoved

the chair back. "There aren't enough bathrooms," she said.

Sam shrugged. "Add some. Put in those Jacuzzi tubs." He said it so easily she nearly dropped the coffee-pot. Two days ago he'd pitched a fit when she suggested installing an electronic lock on the front door.

"Why not put a hot tub in an enclosed gazebo in the backyard? That would be a drawing factor," she murmured. "Don't you think so, Kyle?"

He blinked twice. "You're really serious. I thought you hated restaurant work and, believe me, you'd have plenty of that with a bed and breakfast this size. You said that's why you became an accountant."

"I hated working for my parents. They aren't exactly receptive to new ideas and methods. It was their way or no way. With my own place, I could try out some of those new ideas."

"And fall flat on your face," Kyle pointed out.

She shrugged. "It's my face. My house and my money, too. I'm just beginning to realize what that means, what freedom it gives me."

"Must be nice," Sam agreed. "I, however, have a morning conference to attend. It's neither prudent nor sane to ignore the commands of the department head. See you both later." He stood and ambled out of the house, his shoulders shaking. She hoped he'd make it out of hearing distance before he lost complete control of his laughter.

"About time," Kyle muttered. "Is he over here every morning?" She couldn't detect even a trace of jealousy in his demeanor.

"No," she answered honestly. Usually, she went to Sam's house first thing in the morning. He was the one with the fully functional hot-water heater.

"Good, because I think the guy has a couple of

screws loose. You really should install a security system if you're going to stay here much longer.''

She leaned against the counter. ''I am going to stay, maybe for good.''

Kyle pushed away from the table. ''Hilary, I know you made it plain last night that it's no longer my business, but I can't turn off my feelings that fast. I'm worried about you.''

''Don't. I know what I'm doing.''

''Well, at least I can do some of the groundwork for you before I go back to Chicago. Maybe I'll be able to change your mind.'' He headed for the stairs and the office telephone.

Hilary avoided him for the rest of the day and most of the next. She puttered in the flower beds, even took a couple of long walks in the woods. When she returned from one such walk, she found Sam and Kyle at the kitchen table.

She glanced uneasily from one to the other. ''What's going on?''

''Briggs made you an offer,'' Kyle said.

''I'm not interested.''

''The guy operates on the edge of the law, but he hasn't done anything illegal, at least not that the county attorney can prove,'' Sam said.

''But this morning you said—''

''I checked around a bit today, made some calls while your friend here talked to the man himself.'' He glanced at Kyle with an amiable grin. ''It's a generous offer.''

She shook her head. ''The more I think about it, the more this restaurant idea grows on me. I don't want my land developed in any way or your property, either. That would spoil the ambiance.''

Kyle held up his arms in surrender. ''Go ahead and check out the zoning and mock-up a business plan. See what kind of a bottom line you can expect. If it doesn't look good, you can always go back to the ideas we discussed earlier. Do it on your own if you don't want my help.''

Hilary managed to smile. Her plan wasn't working as well as she'd hoped. She'd have to lay the blarney on thicker. She thumped the wall beside her. "Sam, are you sure this is a load-bearing wall?"

He stepped back, surveying the plastered expanse. "Pretty sure. We could check the blueprints.''

"Blueprints? You must be kidding.''

"If they're the original building plans, they must be worth a fortune as antiques,'' Kyle said.

Sam scratched his chin. "I don't know about their monetary value, but the originals are in the stack Ben and I consulted when we redid the staircase. There was dry rot in the support beams and we had to reinforce them. Having the plans on hand made the job a lot less trouble than it could have been.''

"I didn't find anything like that when I looked through the household accounts,'' she said. Sam's expression was curious, though he didn't say anything. She remembered then that she'd never really explained why she'd suddenly become interested in those old papers.

"They're with his personal papers,'' Sam said. "I think the label on the box says rags or old socks or something like that. Ben figured nobody would be interested in riffling through those.''

"He was right,'' Kyle agreed.

"I'm interested, especially since half the countryside has noticed the family similarities. Maybe I have a double somewhere in the family tree,'' she said, watching Sam. If she had a double, it was her cousin. Too many people had remarked on the likeness.

To her relief, he didn't seem to react at all. She hated

to think that those remarks by his well-meaning friends had reawakened sad memories.

"Let's see if we can find the plans," he said. "It's as good a place as any to start, wouldn't you say so, Kyle?"

Sam started for the stairs without waiting to see who followed.

"Coming, Kyle?"

"No, thanks. Dusty attics aren't my thing. I'll dig through the notes I put together when I started on the subdivision idea and see if there's anything that would apply to a restaurant."

"It's not necessary," she assured him. "You don't owe me anything."

"And vice versa," he said. "I know. I've accepted the fact that you need some time on your own. But humor me. I'll feel better doing what I can to help before I leave."

Hilary touched his arm briefly. "I really want to remain friends, if that's possible."

"We still have a lot in common," he reminded her.

She smiled weakly. "Of course."

It was the truth. And it didn't bode well for any hopes she had concerning Sam, since he and Kyle were opposites. The thought turned her limbs to leaden weights as she climbed the stairs.

"There you are. I was beginning to think you'd changed your mind," Sam called when she finally made it to the attic. He was at the far end, rummaging through a box by the window.

"Did you find them?"

"I'd forgotten how many boxes labeled rags he'd put up here," he said. "Some are the genuine item, too."

It took about fifteen minutes of shuffling and sorting to locate the building plans.

"Unbelievable," she said, spreading the yellowed

sheets on the floor. Newer sheets fluttered down over the old, layer upon layer detailing the addition of the ell in the rear of the house and other minor changes throughout the years.

"Yep, the Neills were great record keepers. Accurate and exacting."

"And I always thought it was just an occupational hazard," she said, laughing easily. "These are amazing. I can't believe they've all survived."

Sam squinted over at her. "Do you really want to knock down walls?"

She shook her head. "The place is pretty much perfect as it is, with a few exceptions in the kitchen."

He smiled. "What are you going to do?"

She eased a step closer, touching his arm. "Actually, the bed and breakfast was a good idea. I don't know about the enclosed gazebo, though." He caught her hand and held it. After Kyle's tense coolness, Sam's easy warmth felt good.

"Historically inaccurate?"

She shook her head. "Too expensive to heat in the winter, too hot in the summer."

He groaned, pulling her closer still. "You're a hopeless case."

"I'd say that's the general consensus," she replied, her voice suddenly husky.

"I have a confession to make," he whispered.

"Oh?"

"I stole your nightgown, that peachy lace thing Kyle was holding when we walked in last night."

Her eyes widened at that. "Why?"

"You didn't miss it?" He looked hopeful.

"Of course, I missed it. I wanted to put it away before Kyle got any more bright ideas."

Sam pulled her closer still, wrapping his arms around her. "Exactly what I thought."

He kissed her lightly, then again. Sweet tenderness flared to passion as she opened her mouth to him, pouring all her frustrations, all her tangled emotion into the kiss. Love had never felt this good before. But this wasn't love. It was rebounding, or lust, or . . . whatever it was, she wanted more.

Her fingers played with the muscles of his shoulders, wonderfully firm muscles that no longer seemed odd on this college professor. They were simply Sam, part of the complex whole she was finding it difficult to resist.

His kneading hand spread heat across her back, down her sides, and beneath the edge of her T-shirt at her midriff. Then they rose higher, spanning her ribs, and higher still to toy beneath the lace edging of her bra.

Hilary groaned, clenching at his arms, not to stop him, but to bring him closer still. She couldn't feel enough of him, taste enough of him. She wasn't even trying to resist him. She didn't want to.

He teased her nipples through the bra. She wished she hadn't worn a padded bra, but rather one of the whisper-thin confections she'd seen at that shop the other day. Or maybe none at all. Definitely none. She'd remember next time.

She heard a gasp, then realized it was her own breathless response as his fingers slipped beneath the confining elastic to cup her breasts. Searing fingers of heat shot through her, and she sought his mouth again. She wanted him. And she could feel his hardness against her, hear his ragged breathing. He wanted her, too.

She slid her hands down his chest, slowly, learning the feel of him. When she touched his belt he stiffened. His hands clasped hers, holding them tightly.

"Do you have any idea what that does to me?"

Hilary stilled, her fingers wrapping themselves

around his of their own accord. He wanted her, yet he'd stopped. Why?

"I'd say it has no effect whatsoever," she said, sounding as unconvinced as she felt. She wanted him to tell her. She knew what touching him did to her. Except she wasn't so sure anymore that the reason was just lust or circumstances or plain proximity. It felt like more.

Sam kissed her again with barely contained passion. The dusty boxes and old trunks seemed to fade away, leaving only the two of them and the sparking fire between them, within them. Then the upper hall clock struck nine, breaking through the haze of Hilary's emotions. She pulled away.

"I'm not sure I'm thinking clearly," she said.

"Me, neither, but who cares when something feels this good," he whispered against her neck. He groaned. "Heck, I care." He pulled back, holding her at arm's length.

She felt the chill of the distance. "What are you saying?"

"I may kick myself for this later, but I'm saying we should wait until both of us are sure. I want you to be sure, because there will be no turning back like with Kyle. This is different. It's too strong to play with."

"I am sure. I—" Hilary began, then her voice died as she spotted Kyle at the top of the narrow staircase, watching her, watching them both. His face was frozen with shock, his color a chalky gray.

ELEVEN

Two weeks later, the look on Kyle's face still haunted her at odd moments. She wished she'd found a better way to convince him she couldn't marry him. She wasn't sure she'd convinced him. But at least he'd gone home. A frown pursed her lips as she remembered his pained expression and the quiet, cold way he'd left.

And then she remembered how Sam had wrapped her in his arms and kissed the chill away. At that moment, she'd known she loved him. The realization hadn't struck like a lightning bolt, but more like the tumblers of a lock clicking into place. It was the answer she'd been seeking.

Yet, she was no closer to knowing what to do about that love than she'd been at the moment of its discovery.

She glanced briefly at the antique covered basket on the car seat beside her and mentally ran through the contents. She'd packed plenty of deli sandwiches, potato salad, and a thermos of iced idea. A linen cloth covered the top, hiding the contents and their too-modern wrappings. She wasn't taking any chances on the nitpicking park director confiscating Sam's lunch because it wasn't historically accurate in either preparation or packaging. And it wasn't, of course, but she'd hidden the evidence, not flaunted it. She was less concerned about her own modern attire since she was just a tourist and not a staff member who was supposed to be setting an example.

She headed through the Missouri Town 1855 main gate and parked at the far end of the gravel lot under the shade of a spreading black walnut tree. She headed for the gift shop as Sam had instructed. The two-story antebellum building reminded her of Sam's house, though this one was smaller.

Inside, a blast of air conditioning hit her, and she allowed herself a small smile. That, at least, was familiar enough. So was the wide central hall, though there was only one room on each side instead of two like at Sam's house. She stepped into a room half-filled with browsing tourists.

"I'm supposed to meet Sam Langford here somewhere," she told a woman dressed in nineteenth century blue cotton. The angular, wrinkled woman peered over her small-framed spectacles and beamed, looking every bit the pioneer storekeeper who'd spotted a visitor bearing news from the East.

"You must be the Neill girl. I'd recognize those eyes and that nose anywhere," the woman said. "Sam said you were coming, and about time, too, if you ask me."

"What do you mean?"

"The man's been up here three times already asking if you've been through. Go on and put him out of his misery," she said, waving away Hilary's money and pressing a postcard-sized visitor's badge into her hand. "Here, he left a pass for you. Tie it onto a button if you have one." She glanced at Hilary's oversized T-shirt and bicycle shorts and sighed. "Hang it on your basket. If anyone says anything, tell them Susan Makepeace said it was fine.''

Hilary let the name pass with barely a lifted brow. It certainly fit her attire and the general spirit of the place, from what Sam had described. He was usually Sam Langford, bachelor carpenter and all-around handyman.

"Where's Sam now?" she asked.

"Probably up at the church, or maybe at the saw pit. They're replacing the church floor. Two of the main support beams had nearly rotted through at one end, and some of the others weren't much better.''

"And the church is?"

"Just go through the gates, honey, and keep on walking. The church is at the bend in the road, a log building bigger than most of the others up that way and built in the shape of a cross.''

Hilary smiled her thanks and headed across the gravel parking lot toward the wooden gates, lingering for a moment at the flower and herb garden near the entrance. Washed out ditches and pastures flanked the road, which dipped down one rolling hill and up another. At the opposite crest, she could see a cluster of buildings. The only things between her and them were split rail fences, cattle, and a few scattered groups of walking tourists.

It wasn't far to the buildings, only a few hundred yards. But the distance helped convey the atmosphere of a pioneer settlement, somewhat isolated and more spread out than she'd imagined. The horse-drawn wagon and the crude saw pit with its flying sawdust and sweaty workers re-enforced the image of another time. So did the period clothing and rustic speech of those who peopled the village and surrounding fields. After a while, Hilary began to feel as if she and the other tourists were the ones out of step.

She found the church with little trouble, though she took great care in skirting a half-loaded wagon drawn by a skittish horse.

"Ah, I see you've brought us lunch," called a sweaty man in a tattered brown vest and baggy tan trousers. A fuzzy red beard hid most of his face, and the drooping brim of his hat shadowed the rest so she couldn't tell whether he was teasing or serious.

"Not exactly," she replied, shifting the heavy basket to her other hand.

He lifted a long, rough sawn plank from the wagon bed and turned, heading toward the church door. The horse snorted and danced, dragging the wagon forward several paces.

"Whoa, there," he called, speaking softly as he grasped the harness and worked his way forward. "Be still now or I'll beat you like a redheaded stepchild."

Sam poked his head out the door. "Watch your mouth, Will. Someday that horse is going to figure out what you're saying." He straightened, wiping his sleeve across his forehead to catch the dripping sweat.

The other man chuckled. "It's all in the tone of voice," he explained. "Don't matter what you say. It's how you say it. Black Bill here is a bit young, not quite settled to the harness yet," he added for Hilary's benefit.

Sam only snorted. "As twitchity as a goose with a fox around the corner," he said, aiming a wink in her direction.

The man ignored him, centering his attention on her. "I lost my wife in a smallpox epidemic back in Tennessee a couple of years ago. Lately I've been lookin' for a new wife. Might you be unwed, ma'am?" His face shone with touching sincerity.

Sam's grin widened. "Mr. Johnson has a large farm just south of town, a small house that needs a little fixing up—" He shot a dubious look at the man. "He mayhaps needs a woman to help him *care* a little more whether the fences are straight and the weeds are pulled in the garden."

"I can't do everything. That's why I need a wife," the man retorted testily, then turned his guileless face back to Hilary. "I have two cows," he declared proudly. "Good milkers, both of them."

Hilary swallowed hard. Then she caught the brief twinkle in the man's eye before he hid it again. This, she decided, was the entertainment that came with the admission price.

"Mr. Johnson," she said, fixing him with the sternest, most prudish expression she could manage. "I'm not in the market for *cows* just now. I will be sure to call on you if I have a need for some extra milk."

"But are you unwed?"

"I am, but I suspect you are perhaps not telling me everything. I was warned that you also have three wild sons who are the scourge of the neighborhood. When I marry, it'll be to a man who wants more than a mother for his undisciplined brats."

"I had a bit more in mind than that," he said defensively.

Beginning to enjoy the game, she pretended horror. "Smelling like you do, of horse and week-old sweat? Talk to me again when you've had a bath."

A broad grin split the man's face as he swiveled to face Sam. "Damn, she's good. Get her some long skirts and put her to work." He winked at her and headed back to the wagon to finish unloading.

She glanced suspiciously at Sam. "Is that why you wanted me to bring lunch, so I could hand you nails and haul boards?"

He shook his head. "That's man's work. You'd be

cooking and washing and tending to the kitchen garden, mayhaps mending a shirt or two.''

Hilary punched him in the arm. "Creep. When's your lunch break?''

"As soon as I help Will unload the wagon,'' he said, already moving in that direction.

While she waited, she sat on the church step on the shady side of the building, reading through the pamphlet about the living history park. All the buildings were authentic, disassembled for moving and reassembled on the site with painstaking care. Even the shingles on the roofs were handmade, using nineteenth century tools and techniques. According to the pamphlet, the entire park was designed to display the daily life of the average person living in Jackson County in the year 1855.

Glancing around, she decided that if it weren't for the tourists, she'd be convinced she'd flown back in time. Sam and his friends put on a believable show. In fact, they were doing the Widower Johnson routine again with another tourist. The gray-haired woman looked shocked, then flattered, though still puzzled. Finally comprehension dawned across her features. The woman realized they weren't insane, that they were playing their parts.

"If you'll pardon me, ma'am,'' Sam said as he dusted his hands on his pants. "I've a young lady waiting for me. We're going to walk down to the lake over yonder and see whether Farmer Johnson's spotted cow has strayed down thataway.''

The man nodded. "I'd be most grateful. I've been meaning to fix that hole in the fence, but the Lord's work comes first,'' he said indicating the stack of lumber next to the church.

Sam and Hilary left him charming the older woman while they headed for the path through the woods.

"I'll bet he has a wife and six kids," Hilary said as they headed toward a narrow cut through the woods.

"Four," Sam said, taking the basket and testing its weight a couple of times. "That's a lot of food. Maybe we should have invited Farmer Johnson along."

"Call him if you want."

"Nope, it's Tuesday."

"And what does Tuesday have to do with it?"

"His wife brings the kids out every Tuesday morning to weed the gardens. They finish up with a picnic lunch before she hauls the brats home."

"A family hobby, huh?"

He turned, stopping on the path. "Sometimes, with some families. Nobody, not even the paid staff, treats this like just another job. That doesn't mean their wives or husbands or the people they're dating feel the same way about it. It isn't a requirement," he said.

She touched the serious furrow in his brow, smoothing it with her fingertips. "I didn't think you meant anything of the sort. I was just asking. So far, I think it's kind of neat here, and very effective as an exhibit of living history, even though I'm not much of a judge since this is the first I've experienced."

"Not quite. I suppose my soldier on the staircase routine would qualify."

She laughed at his rueful expression, then stood on tiptoe to kiss his nose. "This seems painless, though."

He grinned, shaking his head slowly from side to side. "Not in front of the guests, love. Dressed as we are, we're bound to confuse them."

Hilary felt herself blush. She hadn't thought about anyone watching. She'd simply wanted to erase the worry from his face.

"Then let's find a place where they can't see us eat our contraband food and play time-travel kissing games."

He pushed her ahead of him on the path, still holding onto her shoulders. "You want to kiss, huh?"

"All the time," she admitted, glancing back.

He hoisted the basket higher and pushed her faster down the path. "Then move, woman. Stop dillydallying and let's get out of sight."

A moment later, they were hidden in the trees, visible only to anyone coming or going along the path itself. Hilary was thinking of pulling him behind a large oak when she felt a pinch on her derriere.

She screeched, jumping to the side and dodging his outstretched hand. "Why did you do that?"

"I couldn't resist. They were just bouncing around in front of me like two hens in a sack, trying to get out." He shrugged, not looking the least bit repentant. He looked ready to commit the act again, or maybe tweak something else.

"Hens?" Thinking of the fat, fluffy chickens she'd spotted on the other side of the wattle fence, she didn't know whether to be insulted or start running five miles a day.

"Well, maybe small, youngish hens," he said placatingly. He leaned forward, hesitating when she stepped back. "It's that blasted spandex. Did you have to wear those tight shorts? I'm going to have to fight half the men on site just to get you safely back to your car," he said.

She leaned forward, pressing a teasing kiss to his lips, then slipping away before he could shift the basket and hold onto her. "I guess we'd better hurry up and eat so you can build up your strength," she said. She took off down the path, adding a little extra swing to each step.

They found a picnic table down the other side of the hill near the waterfront. A party was in full swing aboard a sailboat anchored nearby in the small cove.

Farther out, two speedboats pulled skiers across the water.

"It seems we aren't alone after all," Hilary said, disappointed. Somehow, she'd envisioned greater seclusion, though she supposed that was a bit naive considering she was at a county lake at the height of summer. "I guess I ought to be grateful there aren't a dozen other picnickers fighting for this table."

"Not here," he assured her. "There's no road or trail except the one we came on. This spot's for park staff."

"A break room by the lake," she filled in. She pulled the cloth from the top of the basket and spread it on the table between them before unpacking the food.

"We spend a lot of time eating together," she commented a while later.

He shrugged. "So? Don't most couples go out to eat a lot?"

"We went out once." He'd finally taken her to the long-awaited Berliner Bear the previous Saturday. "Mostly, we hang around the house, one of them, and cook or raid the refrigerator while we're digging through old junk or fighting it out on the checkerboard." She hadn't decided whether that was good or bad. They were either comfortable with one another or didn't care enough to make the effort. She stared at the sailboat, her mood dampened by that last thought.

"It's cheaper," Sam said after a moment. He caught her chin, forcing her to look at him. "Hilary, do you want to go out more, see a movie, play miniature golf or whatever? I keep forgetting you're accustomed to the pace of a big city."

"Oh, no, I didn't mean I was bored. And I don't need to be wined and dined—"

"Hilary, I don't make a fortune, but I'm not broke either. I can afford to take you about anywhere you want to go." His fingers covered her lips before she could protest. "We could even go Dutch, if you insist. I just didn't realize you missed the night life. You've always seemed to be having fun and you seemed so comfortable with me. I didn't think we needed the other. Maybe we do."

She hesitated, then lowered her gaze to the bone buttons on his shirt. "I don't know whether we're becoming very good friends or . . ." She couldn't say it.

"Or courting?"

"That's one way of putting it."

"Hilary. Look at me." The heat trembling in his tone convinced her she wouldn't find indifference or rejection in his expression. But she didn't expect warlock fire either.

Reaching across the table, he cupped her face with his hands and leaned over to kiss her thoroughly, sweetly, with an implied promise that made her forget any lingering doubts. He leaned back, surveying her with that serious smile that shone only in his eyes.

"Hilary Neill, I'm courting you with *very* serious intentions," he said, his voice husky with emotion.

She couldn't answer at first. So, she kissed him lightly instead. "I'm glad," she finally managed to say.

She packed up the picnic basket in careful silence, savoring the changing tenor in their relationship.

They walked back quickly, making up for time lost lingering over lunch. Mrs. Chandler met them at the church.

"There you two are. Sam, you're wanted up at the office for a meeting. Hilary, sweetheart, I need to ask a favor."

Hilary stood and adjusted her skirts yet again, tucking the blouse into the loose waistband and hitching the skirt higher so she wouldn't trip on the uneven stone steps. She was beginning to see what fun re-enacting could be, but there were definite disadvantages as well, namely these layers of heavy clothes. At least she'd managed to avoid the layers of petticoats some of the other women wore.

When Mrs. Chandler had asked her to fill in for a staff member called away by a family emergency, she'd quickly agreed. The woman had acted so relieved, so grateful. It took Hilary less than an hour to realize how little she knew about anything pertinent to the job of providing information to the visitors. Mrs. Chandler, she suspected, had pulled a scam. And judging from the number of times the woman had sent Hilary to the church on one errand or another, Mrs. Chandler had matchmaking in mind.

Hilary didn't think it necessary to enlighten the woman about her and Sam. And she supposed she was helping simply by being there and dressing appropriately. Imagine that. Hilary Neill was local color—the local klutz in hand-me-down clothes.

When she'd borrowed the clothes, she hadn't thought an extra inch or two at the waist or the hemline could make so much difference. After all, frumpy was frumpy. Now she knew how wrong that idea was, along with a few other long-cherished notions about life in earlier times.

"Honey, I've got a couple of diaper pins tucked in my purse over at the tavern," Mrs. Chandler offered, gesturing vaguely in the direction of the big building across the road. The Chandlers were playing the part of innkeepers for the week. Mrs. Chandler did most of the domestic chores while the old man whittled and entertained the tourists with his stories and colorful explanations about the function of various tools.

Hilary shot her a grateful look. "Maybe I could borrow the pins for a while, if it's allowed. I suppose they have plastic on them." Plastic and all things invented after 1855 were contraband as far as the park director was concerned.

Mrs. Chandler beamed. "Red plastic hearts," she confirmed. "But what that skinny witch doesn't know won't hurt her." Hilary knew the woman referred to the director, though she couldn't see anything wrong with the woman or the way she ran the park site. Susan Makepeace had been friendliness itself. She knew better than to ruffle Mrs. Chandler's features by saying so, though.

"What witch?"

Hilary jumped, startled by Sam's sudden appearance. "Oh, it's you," she said.

"Who's the witch? I didn't hear anything about a witch-burning ceremony at the staff meeting. Are you sure you don't have this place mixed up with Salem?" he teased.

Mrs. Chandler tossed him a tin bucket. "Don't just stand there jawing. Make yourself useful and bring some more water over for Hilary. We'll need several bucketsful for cooking and washing up."

"That's women's work," he protested.

"Are you finished with the church floor?" Hilary parried.

"For today. Will had to leave early, so I don't have any help." He picked up a couple of buckets. "Hilary, you don't have to stay."

"She certainly does," Mrs. Chandler retorted. "If you think I'm going to cook for this crowd by myself, think again. Honey, you wanted to try re-enacting, so you have to stay. There's nothing like cooking over an open fire and then watching ten hungry men eat everything up in nothing flat."

Hilary had to laugh. "I've cooked over an open fire before. Grandpa taught me when we were camping."

"Good, I'll go get those pins while you young folks take care of the water." She gathered up her skirts and hurried across the road toward the tavern, shooing the hens out of her path as she walked.

Hilary turned to Sam. "She must think we don't spend enough time together. She's been playing Cupid all day."

He slid a finger along the length of her jaw. "She's absolutely right."

"I think so, too," Hilary murmured, hiding a smile. She shooed a fly away from the bowl of peeled potatoes, then covered them with a cotton cloth. Handy things, those clothes. She and Mrs. Chandler had used half the stack on the mantle shelf inside the little house. Hilary had even tied one around her hair to hide her modern style.

"Hilary, dear," Mrs. Chandler called from the tavern steps. "Put those in the big pot and set them on the grate. See that your skirts don't get in the fire."

TWELVE

A loud crash in the next room awoke Hilary with a start. She jerked and floundered upright, pushing against the fluffy feather mattress that pillowed around her.

For once, she recognized her surroundings all too clearly. She was still at the park, sleeping alone in the two-room blacksmith's house. And something had disturbed that sleep.

She sat there a moment, probing the stillness for the source of the sound. A faint breeze made a cross wind from the open door at the far end of the house through the open door beside the bed. It fluttered through the thin cotton of her borrowed shift, cooling her heated skin. The moonlight shone brightly again tonight, beaming through the opened door to pool on the worn floorboards.

Something skittered across the floor in the next room. It sounded like a very large rat, then more tiny feet joined the dance, scratching against the wood floor. She remembered the pie she'd left cooling in the tin-punch cabinet and bolted out of the bed. Damned if she'd let a herd of mice nibble on that pie after all the trouble she'd gone to make it.

She hurried into the next room. Something furry brushed past her and she jumped back, shrieking with surprise and distaste. Mice? That had been too big to be a mouse. She edged across the room to the pantry, intending to check the damage. But she forgot about the low stool by the fireplace. She stubbed her toe and shrieked again, this time with pain and fury. Sliding down the wall, she grasped the throbbing toe. She found herself staring into the masked face of a large raccoon. Balancing on its haunches, it grasped a polished teaspoon between two furry paws. The raccoon hissed, then released a trilling, growling sound. Three matching masks in miniature crept past her and headed for the bedroom, and hopefully out the door.

No such luck. First one, then the next trotted across the streak of moonlight that split the room and began rustling around under her bed. Hilary released a growl of her own and grabbed the broom, batting it around.

The mother raccoon hissed, showing wicked-looking teeth in the moonlight. She swiped a clawed paw at the broom, then called her youngsters with low chitterings. She ushered them outside, leading them nonchalantly down the steps.

She slammed the door behind the creatures, then ran to the other side to close that door, too. She leaned against it, her heart pounding from the adrenaline surging through her body. If her toe didn't hurt so badly, she'd think she was still asleep and dreaming. But this was unbelievably, ridiculously real.

She slid to the floor, overtaken by a fit of laughter. In all those years of camping with her grandfather, she'd never had an encounter with a wild animal to match this. It was like something out of an old Disney movie, the kind that featured slapstick animal comedy. Life certainly hadn't been dull lately.

"Hilary?" Sam tapped lightly on the bedroom door. "Are you all right?"

Afraid he would wake someone in one of the other buildings, she hurried to open the door. "Couldn't be better," she managed, speaking between fits of giggles. She stepped aside, giving him room to enter.

"I see you've had visitors," Sam said, watching her carefully.

"Four." It was more of a squeak than a word. Feeling silly for giggling like a teenager, she returned to the kitchen and crouched to clear the mess. She could see an overturned fruit bowl, scattered biscuits left from dinner, and a broken piece of crockery. Bright as the moonlight was, it didn't reach the shadowed area under the table or in the corners.

"I'm glad to see you're taking this well," Sam said.

"I'm sorry," she said. "I'll stop in a minute. Did I wake anyone else?"

"I don't think so. I was close by or I wouldn't have heard either.

"They left a mess," he commented. He bent to retrieve the spoon the raccoon had dropped. He glanced sideways at her, holding up an apple with one side chewed out. That only made everything seem even funnier. She could barely breathe for laughing so hard.

"This is funny?" He straightened, moving carefully toward her.

She nodded, then clasped her hands over her mouth, trying to regain control. He probably thought she was hysterical, but it would take more than a raccoon family to put her in that condition. After all, she'd saved the pie and God only knows what other booty the furry bandit and her offspring had their eyes on.

"She hissed at me like I was invading *her* space."

"The coon? She could have bitten you. You should have left or called me."

"And let her get that pie?"

"Think about it, was it worth it?"

She nodded, then drew a deep breath, fighting the laughter that hadn't subsided yet. "I can't believe I defended a pie with a broom," she muttered.

"I know. I saw you when I was climbing over the fence," he explained, chuckling himself. "Brave little buggers, weren't they, taking you on like that. They're lucky you only had a broom and not a load of sheets to throw over the poor, unsuspecting animals," he said, his voice laced with humor.

"You make me sound like a disaster waiting to happen."

"No, just a lady who knows how to take care of herself," he said, allowing a pregnant pause. "Most of the time."

She sensed the change in him, the husky lilt his voice had taken on. And she was suddenly conscious of how little she really wore, of how little he wore.

Moonbeams, distorted by the wavy, old window glass, threw rippled light on his face and across his bare chest. She decided she'd never have curtains as long as Sam remained in her life. He wore only a pair of loose trousers she'd washed early in the afternoon in the big tub right behind this house. That bit of drudgery took on shades of intimacy.

Her cool, cotton shift was suddenly too thin, exposing too much. A shiver that had nothing to do with chill ran up her spine. She could feel the heaviness of her breasts, the faint brush of the cloth against their raised nipples. She crossed her arms to hide them from his gaze.

"Your chivalry steals my breath," she said. She turned purposefully toward the window, looking across the road toward the tavern full of sleeping people. "You're sure no one else heard."

"I don't see anyone else coming." He moved so close she could feel the heat radiating from his bare chest to her back. "I guess they're all sleeping soundly."

"Why weren't you?" The question echoed in the stillness, stretching between them. This had happened before, the two of them awake beneath the stars while everyone except the night creatures slept.

"Mr. Chandler snores. I'd just moved my bedroll over near the stable to get away from the noise. I can't imagine how his wife sleeps through it."

"Ear plugs?" Hilary suggested, frowning into the night. It hadn't been snoring that had kept him awake those other nights.

"You know," he said, gently turning her around. "We have to stop meeting like this." His voice had grown serious, husky with longing.

The moonlight still highlighted the curling hairs on his chest, but fell short of revealing his expression. He could hide so much in those shadows.

"Or do something about it," she answered, barely above a whisper.

He stepped toward her, pulling her into his arms and himself into the full moonlight. His hungry eyes watched her, waiting for something she couldn't fathom. She tangled her fingers in his hair, urging his lips closer until he groaned and captured her mouth in a devastating kiss. There was no subtlety in the way he moved against her, but that wasn't what she wanted right now. His tongue traced her lips, demanding entrance. She gave freely, meeting each teasing thrust with fiery passion until he moaned with pleasure. And still he demanded more. She lost track of time and space. Her head was spinning and only her arms around

Sam's neck kept her from swaying, from buckling at the knees and falling to the floor.

His breathing was as harsh as hers when they came up for air. She felt fevered, her breasts swollen and aching for his touch. She brushed against him until he groaned and held her still.

"I want to make love with you," he said.

Her heart turned over. "I want you, too," she whispered, punctuating each word with a teasing kiss along his jaw.

His arms around her tightened. "Wanting isn't enough. I have to have everything about you, body and soul."

She gasped, her breath catching in her throat at the sincerity quivering in his tone. Possession and desire warred for dominance in his steady gaze. His message was clear. If she took him to her bed, he'd own her. He wanted her soul, but he'd offered only his body. She teetered on the brink of indecision, weighing her desire, her love against her need for his love in return.

He slid gentle hands down her back, tracing the curve of her spine, then spreading to cup her derriere. He lifted her, holding her tight against him so she could feel the evidence of his desire.

"Feel me," he said. "Feel what you do to me and decide now while I am still capable of stopping." His eyes pinned her. She met them with a boldness beyond anything she'd known before. She'd been lost in those eyes too long to change her mind now.

"Love me," she answered.

Passion, triumph, raw desire, and tenderness chased one another across his face until a measure of each mingled in his expression. He lifted her higher, cradling her against him as he strode the remaining steps through the doorway into the bedroom. She traced a trail of warm kisses along his collarbone, then felt the feather mattress around her once again as he lay her gently down. She started to sit up, to reach for the buttons at his waistband. He eased her back down with stroking fingers that teased her sensitive flesh. Hot shivers shook her body and seduced her thoughts until she ceased to think. She could only feel, float in the sensual spell he'd cast over her body.

He untied the ribbon at the gathered neckline of the shift, then slipped the thin fabric over her shoulders and down until it gathered around her waist. Calloused fingers lightly caressed her shoulders, then skimmed along her rib cage, teasing the rounded sides of her breasts. His thumbs worked in decreasing circles until they traced the peaked nubs. Then his lips traced the path of his fingers until she cried out, clenching her own impatient fingers to his shoulders.

"Did I hurt you?" He paused, his breath fanning her sensitized nipple.

"Just the opposite," she declared, rolling sideways to give her searching fingers greater access to his magnificent body. The feather mattress lumped beneath her and she shifted again, sliding into the valley made by the imprint of their bodies. She matched him touch for touch, exploring kiss to teasing caress until she'd learned the feel of every inch of his strong back, of the firm expanse of his chest.

When she fumbled with the trouser buttons, he helped her. He playfully tugged first the gown and then her sensible cotton panties down over her hips. She shivered again. He covered her body with his own, letting the hard warmth of him stoke the fire burning in her belly until she squirmed restlessly against him, her lips demanding his. And still he caressed, teasing her belly, brushing even lower, skimming her hips and down the length of her smooth, firm legs. He found the sensitive spot behind her knee and kissed it, then moved higher until she jerked with surprise at the shocking touch of his tongue. Mind-drugging pleasure radiated through her limbs, feeding the tension building inside her to a fever pitch.

"I want you," he whispered.

She wrapped her legs around him in answer, urging him closer to the ultimate intimacy. And then he was inside her, filling her, dragging her soul from her. She heard a voice in the distance, then realized it was her, calling his name over and over until he covered her mouth with his own and captured her pleasured cries.

She felt him stiffen and jerk. Her world exploded around her, within her. Sensations she'd never imagined shuddered through her, whirling, floating, trembling orgasmic sensations.

"I love you," she whispered against his lips, then surrendered once more to his kiss.

Slowly, reality filtered back in the form of feathery, soothing touches, soft night sounds floating through the open window, and Sam's steady breathing. He shifted, cradling her against him spoon fashion while he nuzzled her neck.

"Stay with me," he whispered.

"I'm not going anywhere. This is my bed for the night," she reminded him. She could feel his breath on the nape of her neck, fanning delicious sensations, heat and chill tremors mixed into one.

"I don't mean just tonight," he said.

Her heart tripped a beat, then steadied. He rolled over, propping up on his elbows above her, touching her sated body with the length of him. And she felt the passion stir anew.

"Stay with me," he repeated. "Don't go back to Chicago. Come live with me in my home or in yours, and make love with me all night, every night."

"You tempt me," she answered. She felt a strange

foreboding as she touched the moonstruck highlights in his hair, wishing she could see his shadowed expression. But his features were hidden from the moonlight. She had only his words. She'd declared her love. He'd declared his desire. He'd asked for her soul and she'd given it.

"Will you still want me when the day comes, when we're not lying together in the aftermath?"

He kissed her with a tenderness that soothed her fears. "Hilary Neill, when you walked into my life, you brought the light back with you. I need your light more than I need air to breathe," he said.

She couldn't speak because of the tears welling up. When one escaped, stealing down her cheek, she didn't even try to stop it. "I love you," she said, her voice shaking with emotion. "And I don't say that lightly. I left Kyle for you, the man I'd planned to marry."

"Regrets?"

"No." She was sure of that. She could almost regret having hurt Kyle, but the more she thought about it, the more she realized he'd brought it on himself. If he'd made her a priority, she might not have been ripe for Sam's charms. "I think I made a good trade," she added after a moment.

"Do you now, woman?"

"I might need more convincing." She trailed teasing fingers down his back, over his hips. He crushed her to him, rolling over and balancing her on top of him, laughing too loudly in his jubilation.

"Shhh," she whispered. "You'll wake everyone."

"I don't care. Let's tell them now.

Hilary giggled. "Let's not. Let's keep this to ourselves for awhile."

His laughter died. "Why? You aren't sure."

She laid a quieting finger across his lips. "I love you, Sam Langford, and I want to be with you," she affirmed. She snuggled up against him, ignoring the faint sense of foreboding that seeped into her consciousness when he didn't answer, but simply clutched her tightly against him.

I want to be with you, marry you, bear your sons and daughters to race through the hallways and shout beneath the trees of Neill House.

But he hadn't said marry. Maybe he thought it was too soon for her. Maybe he still needed time to get used to the two of them, to understand that beneath the passion was a firm foundation for sharing a life together. Opposites do attract, and blend, and meld.

She was his light.

So what if he hadn't said the words she wanted most to hear.

A heavy weight held Hilary's eyelids closed as the deep, black void of sleep beckoned her back under its spell. Well, not completely void. The vague outline of a dream lingered, a dream of her and Sam sharing a clandestine kiss on the path to the lake. Savoring the memory, she stretched, then snuggled sleepily against the warmth beside her. Something brushed against her cheek. The sensation intermingled with her dream, teasing her closer to wakefulness.

She eased her leg closer to Sam's warmth. The shape she encountered didn't feel quite right. Raising on one elbow, she blinked in the dimness. The warm shape beside her was nothing more than a feather pillow atop a lump in the mattress.

She was alone.

Outside, the dawn lit pink streaks across the sky. The rest of the village still slept. Not even the creaking of crickets or a snort from the nearby sheep pen disturbed the silence. She supposed she should be grateful he had the presence of mind to leave before the others arose, sparing them the speculative looks and curious comments of the others. Instead, she simply felt bereft and not a little disappointed. The faint morning light she'd always thought rosy and full of promise only seemed to mark the close of a night she didn't want to end. Then she saw it, tangible evidence that she hadn't been alone.

At the edge of the mattress closest to the opened window lay a large, trumpet-shaped flower. It looked suspiciously like a pumpkin blossom from the nearby vegetable garden. She picked it up, touching the fragile, orange tissue that hadn't begun to wilt yet. A drop of cool morning dew dampened her finger and touched off a pang of emotion deep within her. Sam had left it for her so she wouldn't feel abandoned when she awoke.

She sank back against the feather mattress, cradling the blossom at her breastbone between her cupped hands. She stared at the ceiling, her thoughts drifting through sultry memories and new dreams for the future. Sam cared for her. He'd spoken of a permanent future.

Hilary wanted permanence, roots, and all the trappings. They'd marry, then live in Neill House's high-ceilinged rooms—he loved Neill House. She knew he'd choose that over the one he lived in now. They'd make love in the big bed in the corner room, raise children in the Neill tradition. She frowned. They hadn't discussed children. They'd scarcely talked. Her smile returned. They'd been busy with other things.

She awoke some time later, faintly surprised that she'd slept again. The small sounds of a community stirring to life pricked at her consciousness, urging her out of bed. She dropped the wilting blossom into a cup of water, then quickly dressed in the costume she'd worn the day before. She finished none too soon.

"Hilary, sweet? You awake?" Mrs. Chandler called through the kitchen window.

"Be right there." Hilary tucked the haywire wisps of hair under the tied flour sack cap and grabbed a bar of soap from the cupboard before she opened the door. A quick wash would wipe the last of the sleep from her eyes.

Mrs. Chandler cast an approving eye over Hilary's attire. "Well, you look none the worse for your night's adventures," she said.

Hilary turned away to hide the hot flush flaming across her face. "What do you mean?" Even embarrassment couldn't stop the lingering sense of exhilaration.

The older woman chuckled as she began rustling about in the cupboards. "Sam's already told us about your visitors. Said you chased them out with a broom and slammed the doors before he could come to help you. For a city woman, you're not doing too badly."

Hilary drew a deep breath of relief. So, he'd already given them the edited version of the night's events. "They were not getting that pie," she declared, bending to retrieve a fork she'd missed when hampered by the night's shadows.

Another chuckle shook the woman's ample front. "It's a good thing none of the men decided to snitch that pie like they threatened yesterday. They'd be waking up in the hospital about now."

Hilary grinned. "I'd have to use something heavier than a broom."

Mrs. Chandler pointed to the poker propped against the fireplace and winked.

Light bubbling laughter escaped from Hilary's lips. "That might work." She picked up the last of the raccoon's handiwork, then hesitated. A bit of carved wood stuck out from beneath the tall pie safe in the corner. Hilary grasped it and carefully pulled out a small, framed needlepoint picture.

"Very nice," she observed as she brushed dust from the finely stitched silks. "I wonder how long that's been down there?"

Mrs. Chandler glanced over, then beamed. She set the stack of pots back into the cupboard and reached out to take the picture. "I'd wondered where Sarah's stitchery got to," she said.

Hilary's startled gaze flew back to the needlework. *Sarah's stitchery?* The framed work depicted a pastoral scene, a bonneted woman working in a garden. It could have been any garden—or the one behind the house. Hilary glanced at the older woman, wondering if she dared ask if the needlewoman was the same Sarah who had stitched those beautiful seats for the dining room chairs. She didn't know why she suddenly felt so apprehensive. So, she'd made magnificent love last night with the man who had once been Sarah's husband. So, she'd lusted after him weeks before while lying in Sarah's marriage bed. It had no bearing on the present, right? After all, Sarah died seven years ago.

"My second cousin, Sarah?" Hilary finally asked as nonchalantly as she could manage.

"Yes, she did such beautiful work," Mrs. Chandler said. It's kind of a tradition to leave something to mark your stay if you've slept overnight here. She stitched this the first Living History Week we had here. She made the frame, too, though not until after she'd gone back home." Mrs. Chandler polished the frame with the cloth of her clean apron, then held it up to the light, apparently unaware of Hilary's turmoil. "I haven't seen this in months. I figured Sam took it home or maybe someone stole it."

Hilary rearranged the fruit in the burl bowl on the table while she considered the implications. "Sam and Sarah slept here?"

Mrs. Chandler straightened, turning perceptive gray eyes on Hilary. "Years ago, yes."

Hilary tried to smile. "Of course," she said, starting toward the door. "I'll be back in a few minutes. I need to wash up before we start breakfast."

She hurried down the path toward the public restrooms, the only place on the site with running water. Her thoughts were elsewhere, though, lost in memories made on the feather mattress that was too big for a woman alone, yet marvelously accommodating for the two of them.

But what other memories did Sam have of that big feather bed?

THIRTEEN

It was time he did something about this house, Sam decided as he stared thoughtfully around the central hall, waiting for the plumber to finish repairing the horrendous leak that had flooded the cellar. It seemed that leaks, like other forms of bad luck, came in threes. Two for Hilary, one for him. As a couple, that made three.

He chuckled ruefully to himself, blaming the giddy thought on the odd euphoria that struck him every time he thought of her.

"That about wraps it up for now," Randy grumbled as he cleared the cellar door hidden behind the staircase.

Sam grimaced at the wet footprints the man left through the hall. Times like these, he regretted giving in to Sarah and replacing the outdoor stairs with indoor ones.

"How much do I owe you?" was all he said aloud and added what he hoped was a grateful smile.

Randy hesitated, then rubbed his chin. "That depends on whether you fix it piecemeal or spring for the whole redo now."

"Exactly what are you suggesting?" Sam asked, easing himself to his feet. There on the stairs, he towered over the stocky man, who was a head shorter than Sam, anyway. Even so, he felt at a distinct disadvantage. Plumbing was his weak point when it came to restoration work.

"Well," the man began, rocking on his heels as he drew out the word. "You have three more spots that could break open any time. I'd advise you replace all the cast-iron pipes before that happens."

"How much will it cost?"

Randy smiled. "Not half as much as it would if you keep calling me out here to fix the breaks one at a time."

"And the work you did today?"

"Since you're in a hurry, I'll just send you a bill," the man conceded. "I'll throw an estimate for the rest in with it."

Sam hid a grin as he nodded his agreement, then waved the man out the door. Some concession. The man probably would end up with four times the amount of today's bill by the time the job was done. He could afford to be accommodating.

Sam sighed heavily. It wasn't just the leak that bothered him. Sure, the new paint had brightened the exterior, not to mention extending the life of the pine-clapboard siding. But inside, his home was still seedy and faded, with stains on the wallpaper and scratches in the woodwork. When Ben was alive, Sam had lavished too much time on Neill House while neglecting his own. Then Hilary came along and threw his priorities into disarray once again.

He didn't regret a single second. Still, he needed to finish this house. It was every bit as old as the other, though not nearly so grand. He tapped his chin thoughtfully. Everything hinged on her. If she stayed with him, where would she want to live? It might make a difference whether they were restoring for themselves or for a tenant. Or a new owner.

Frowning, he stroked the worn banister. He hadn't considered that before. He couldn't imagine strangers living here, fixing what he should have fixed long ago, redoing the wallpaper Sarah had so lovingly hung. The place was every bit as embodied with memories as Neill House.

Neill House had always been the issue, not his own home. At first, he hadn't thought beyond diverting Hilary from any course that would damage the historical masterpiece he and Ben had restored. Now, he couldn't escape the lingering sense of awe that this woman had rescued him from the emptiness of his busy life. She said she loved him, and he welcomed the changes, most of them at least. He was still anxious about her plans for Neill House, but that had paled in importance as he gradually fell in love with her.

"And maybe she has ideas of her own," he muttered, half afraid of what they might be. He still hadn't recovered from the shock over the restaurant scheme, even though it had only been a ploy to send Kyle on his way.

Maybe he should ask her about the two houses tonight. No, that was presuming too much. He didn't want to muddy tonight's celebration with the problem. Tonight was hers. Theirs. He picked up the flat jeweler's box from the hall table and smiled. It wasn't what he wanted most to give her, but he feared she wasn't ready to wear his ring, not when she'd just shed Kyle's. Nevertheless, he wanted to ask her so badly that he thought of little else.

The necklace was a compromise between his needs and his sense of decency. Cleaned and restringed, it was his gift to the woman he loved, a gift that shouldn't have to be a gift. It was hers by right, but this was the only way he could think of to persuade her to accept it. It seemed very important that she do so. He'd tried before and failed. This time, he'd gauge the atmosphere, then offer it as an engagement present or a congratulatory gift to celebrate the job she'd been offered in Kansas City yesterday. Either way, she couldn't refuse.

He'd wait until after dinner, then slip it around her neck and kiss the irresistible curve at the nape. He allowed himself a moment's indulgence in the sensual fantasy of what might happen next.

The fantasy still lingered on the fringes of his imagaintion as he slipped quietly into Hilary's house. He hesitated for a moment in the enclosed back porch, savoring the mingled sensations of spicy aromas, off-key humming, and the sweet fire of anticipation. He tapped the jeweler's box for luck, then crept to the doorway.

"What do you say we skip dinner?" he said, speaking softly so as not to startle her.

She jumped anyway, dropping the wooden spoon to the floor. "Don't do that!" she said, pretending anger.

He didn't believe it for an instant, though, not when the tiny lines around her eyes crinkled into a smile. She came toward him, and he saw the heated flicker behind her welcome. He set the jeweler's box carefully out of sight behind a flowerpot of greenery on the counter before folding her into his arms. It wouldn't do to spoil the surprise before the moment was ripe.

The familiar lump rose in his throat, revealing more than he'd like in the huskiness of his voice. "Like I said—"

"Not a chance. Not when I've been slaving over a hot stove for hours."

He raised a brow as she melted into his arms. "You were at my house an hour ago," he reminded her.

Her quick kiss tasted of tomatoes and oregano. "An hour and a half, but who's counting? Did Randy clean out your life savings?"

Sam's groan was real. "Not yet, but he has plans to. That wasn't the only bad length of pipe down in the cellar, just the worst. He says all the drain lines need replacing."

Hilary scowled sympathetically. "That does sound expensive. Is this something you might do yourself?"

"A wise man knows his limitations."

Her smile was warm and inviting. "How long will your plumbing be out of commission?"

"Excuse me?"

"Well, you opened your house and your bathroom to me when we were barely on speaking terms. Returning the favor is the least I could do, especially now that we're more friendly," she said.

"Should I pack a suitcase?" He chuckled, pretending he wasn't as serious as he felt.

The invitation in her eyes turned to heated promise. "That sounds like a good idea, but a bit melodramatic considering you only live across the road."

"And use my place for a closet? That's a heck of a closet, even for the consort of an heiress," he said.

"Consort?" She shrieked with laughter, but he didn't know whether its source was the word or his fingers tickling her ribs. She backed up, laughing as she slapped his hands away.

"Stop it," she squealed. "You're nuts, you know that?"

He shrugged, pasting on his best little-boy smile. "Nuts about you," he said. "Since the first moment I saw you."

A shadow crossed her face briefly, then she laughed,

though not so lightly as before. "You thought I was a ghost." She didn't need to be more specific. The dimming of her exuberance told him she hadn't forgotten.

"I did not," he insisted. "Well, maybe just for a split second before my common sense told me that wasn't possible."

"Then you thought I was a burglar."

Now she was humoring him, watching him with the tolerant expression that indicated she knew exactly what he would say next. He changed mental gears.

"That's when I fell for you," he said.

It was her turn to groan. "That is the worst pun I've ever heard. I think you'd better feed your brain before it shuts down from lack of nourishment." She returned to the stove, glancing around for the spoon.

He retrieved it from beneath the table and handed it over to her. So what if he'd made the worst joke in the history of mankind. It had brought the sparkle back to her eyes. The ghost was banished once more.

She flushed under his scrutiny and tried to pretend amusement. "Shut up and try this. I think it needs something," she said, holding a spoon dripping reddish sauce.

"What is it, spaghetti sauce?"

She shook her head. "An old family recipe. It goes over beef and potatoes. Come on, try it."

He tasted it, savoring the pungent flavor. It was unique, with the faintly sour bite reminiscent of sauerkraut, yet not unpleasant. He caught her anxious stare.

"It's wonderful just as it is," he said. She was making him delirious and nervous at the same time.

She rolled her eyes at him. "I think there's too much oregano. Remind me next time, and I won't use as much. Do you want to start on the salad while the rest finishes cooking?" She frowned down into the pot and stirred again.

Sam didn't think he could swallow, let alone eat. It wasn't her fault. His own thoughts, his intentions made him almost as nervous as the fear that tonight might not work out as he'd hoped.

To hell with setting the stage. He'd done that for weeks. He couldn't wait any longer.

He plucked the spoon from her hand and dropped it back into the pot, then flicked the stove knobs, turning the burners off. With a low growl, he swept her into his arms and headed for the staircase.

Hilary curled her arms around his neck. "What are you doing?"

"Sweeping you off your feet, you stubborn wench," he retorted, stopping an instant for a quick, hard kiss that left him breathless. He'd better not do that again. He'd never make it up the stairs. He'd never considered that before, making love on the stairs, maybe on the landing. Kinky, if not dangerous.

"That's a naughty smile," she observed. One well-placed kiss at the corner of his mouth destroyed his good sense. He set her down, pinning her against the newel post and followed up on the promise of her soft touch. Her moist, parted lips just beckoned him to do his damndest to make her forget everything except him.

Instead, she stole his every thought, every one except the very real, very urgent need to make love to her. She *would* be his.

"Oh, heck," he muttered as he came up for air. "Wait here for me. No, come with me."

"What?"

"I want to do this right. Humor me, please." He kissed her tenderly, pleading with his gentleness.

She looked touched and more than a little puzzled. "All right, if it's that important to you."

"It is." Taking both hands, he pulled her back to

the kitchen and retrieved the flat box from behind the planter.

"What's that?" She eyed the box warily, as if she was afraid of the contents. Or was disappointed.

Maybe she'd anticipated something else. Maybe he should have gotten the ring after all. His instinct was to respond with sarcasm, covering his uncertainty with laughter. However, he didn't want to cheapen the sentiment, especially not when her expression changed, giving her eyes that luminous look. He could drown in those eyes and never know the difference.

"Here, in the dining room." He flicked on the switch, throwing the room into crystalline prisms of light from the chandelier. "Close your eyes." He kissed the closed lids with reverence, then drew a deep breath.

"Keep them closed," he reminded her, then eased her over to face the resilvered mirror with the Neill crest of intertwining oak leaves and acorns carved into the frame. The mirror reflected them both, her smooth, lovely face and his intent, overly eager expression as he watched from over her shoulder. He popped open the box, touching the smooth orbs that gleamed with warm, ivory iridescence against the velvet lining. *Was he doing the right thing?* He prayed she'd understand, that he could find the right words.

He started to drape the strand around her neck, then hesitated, frowning at the buttoned-up blouse she wore. She ought to be wearing silk and lace, not plain old cotton. He dropped the pearls onto the buffet and undid her top button.

"Sam?" Her startled exclamation made him hesitate.

He kissed her and undid the second button. "In a minute, you'll see. Trust me?"

She nodded, fluttering her lids closed. When he touched the third button, her faint gasp nearly undid him. He nudged the blouse open, pulling the fabric away from her neck, over the curve of her shoulders to rest on her upper arms.

"Gives off-the-shoulder a whole new meaning," she said in a thready voice. Her eyes remained closed. Trust. He wanted to stop time and savor the feel of it for awhile. But time wouldn't stop, and she wouldn't wait much longer. On second thought, he was the one who couldn't wait.

"Marry me," he whispered. His heart plummeted to his stomach as her eyelids flew open. He swallowed, trying to dislodge the lump in his throat. He'd done it all wrong.

"What did you say?" Hope flickered across her face, giving him the courage to continue.

"Marry me," he repeated to the image in the mirror because he was too afraid to turn her around and face the real woman. "Live with me. Love with me."

She smiled, and the sunshine returned to his soul. "Oh, Sam, I do love you." She twisted in his arms and kissed him full on the lips, a kiss of passion and promise and pleasures to come.

"This is the oddest proposal I've ever heard of," she said after a moment. "Why the blouse routine? Softening me up?" Teasing mischief danced in her eyes.

He lifted the pearl strand, draping it around her neck. "For you," he said. He pulled her closer while he wrestled with the stiff catch, which was a challenge for his shaking fingers. Finally, he managed to fasten it. He kissed her again, then turned her toward the mirror.

It was like watching all her blood drain to her toes. She stared at him, her gray eyes standing out sharply against the ghostly white of her skin. Damn, he'd done this badly. He tried again.

"I looked at rings, then I was afraid you weren't ready, that you'd say no," he admitted. "Then I remembered these."

Hilary squeezed her eyes closed. Her skin felt ice cold to his touch.

"These should be yours," he said anxiously. "I tried to give them to you before."

"Sarah's pearls," she whispered, stricken. "The ones in your wedding picture."

He hadn't thought of them that way in a long time, hadn't considered she would. He shook his head. "The Neill pearls, handed down from mother to eldest daughter for six generations. Since you're the last in line, I thought I'd do the honors."

She drew a deep, pained breath and stepped out of his arms. She sank into the chair at the end of the table, away from the mirror. For a moment, she seemed to look right through him, then her eyes focused. The hurt look in them twisted his gut.

"I can't marry you," she said, her voice calm and even.

He knelt next to her. He'd made a grave mistake, but he could correct it. He'd do anything to wipe the pain from her face.

"I'm sorry. I should have waited. I should have realized it's too soon." Finally, her staying hand on his arm registered.

She shook her head. "I can't take Sarah's place. I won't try." She reached behind her neck and unclasped the necklace with a single fluid motion. The skill of it surprised him, and his mind latched onto the action like a drowning man grabs a log. Nimble fingers. Talented fingers on a talented woman, though her skills were mostly the kind he did not understand or have himself.

"I don't understand."

She didn't answer for a long moment. When she did, her voice was clear and as brimming with sadness as her shimmering storm-cloud eyes. "Sarah's pearls. You loved her very much and she died. I look a lot like her, and I think that's what attracted you in the first place. We seem to be doing all the same things the two of you did together, working on the house, reenactment, even sleeping in the same bed at the park.''

Sam felt ill as comprehension seeped through his thick skull. ''That's not why I fell in love with you. You're not at all like her.''

''I wish I could believe you, but there are too many things.''

''Like what? I don't call you by her name. I haven't made our home a shrine. Damn it, I got on with my life a long time before you came here.''

''You still carry her picture, don't you?''

He hesitated. ''I carry one of you now, too. We have a future together if you'll let us. But our future doesn't erase our pasts. Our pasts have made us who we are.''

Hilary sat there. Suddenly, she just looked tired, almost drained of all the vibrancy that was her. He tried to be angry with her, but she looked so lost.

''I love you,'' he said, wishing he had the words to make it right. ''Just you. The pearls were a mistake. I just didn't think, didn't even consider that you would react this way.''

She grasped his hand, squeezing it. ''Oh, Sam. I wish I could be enough for you. Now, if you'll excuse me.'' She dropped the pearls into his palm and curled his lifeless fingers around them. She rose swiftly from the chair and left the room. He heard her soft footfalls running on the stairs. He wanted to call to her, to urge her to be careful, to slow down lest she fall. But he couldn't force the words past the pain lodged like a physical obstruction in his throat.

How could he have made such a mistake?

He headed for the stairs, hoping to right the wrong before it was too late, before she was forever lost to him.

FOURTEEN

Hilary found the pearls on the kitchen counter the next morning when she went in search of mind-clearing caffeine. The pearls lay with a note atop a stack of odd-sized, bound volumes, positioned strategically in front of the coffeepot.

She hesitated, tempted to turn around and go back upstairs. She didn't want to know what Sam had written. She'd already heard it all. What good would it do to rehash it?

She did want to know. She picked up the note.

Read them. If you can read the truth that Ben wrote and still leave, then you're not the woman I thought you were. If you won't believe me, then at least give Ben a chance.

Curious, she lifted the top volume, then hesitated. Weeks ago, Sam had offered them, but she'd been too busy to read them. This time, he'd left them like a chocolate bar on Christmas Eve for Santa. Hilary didn't care for the tactic. She didn't like being manipulated. She grimaced, slamming the book to the counter with surprising force. The action knocked the pearls to the floor with a loud clatter.

Hilary gasped at her own violence. Slowly, she bent to retrieve the strand and check it for damage. It seemed intact, but that didn't lessen her horror at what she'd done. The necklace was priceless. She could never wear it, but she didn't want it destroyed. She couldn't destroy something this beautiful simply because the sight of it reminded her of the woman she couldn't compete with.

A sob caught in her throat as she slipped the pearls back into the jeweler's box. The tears that had eluded her the night before finally broke free.

She cried until dry, racking hiccoughs replaced the tears. When those faded, she sat quietly in the corner feeling completely drained.

Read them. Another order in a long string of orders, pleas, and various requests that all meant the same thing. Trust me. Believe me. She did believe Sam in everything except this. Sam couldn't see, though, what she'd finally understood.

He didn't want *her*. Any brown-haired woman with the Neill chin would do.

"Why am I not enough? Me, not the ghost. No, damn it, damn it. I am enough. He's the fool," she muttered. At least in the light of day, though, she could admit to a very human failing. She'd been too blindly in love to see the truth.

Two blind fools. Maybe they deserved each other.

"Wrong." Saying it aloud made it more convincing. Even if it hurt worse than anything she'd ever experienced, she had to keep her distance. She deserved better than a lifetime as a stand-in for a cousin she'd never met, the canonized dead wife.

Sam had denied it, of course, first through her closed bedroom door and then to her face when he'd knocked the bedroom door down. It said something for the strength of his obsession that he'd damaged a piece of

Neill House in his effort to make her listen. And she had listened, until the words swirled around in confusing circles, until anger overrode the shock of it, and she'd ordered him from the house. Despite the words, though, she couldn't deny what she'd finally understood, even if he refused to face it.

Sam wanted Sarah, but he couldn't have her, at least not in this lifetime. But Hilary Neill was as close a substitute as he was likely to find. If he married her, he'd have both Neill House and a wife who looked much like the woman he'd loved and lost.

She should have seen this coming, but she'd been too blindly in love to recognize the signs. The clues had been there from their first meeting to the magical night they'd made love in that feather bed, the bed where he'd slept with Sarah all those years ago.

Hilary had come here to get her thoughts together, to make a few important decisions. In that sense, her trip had succeeded. In the larger sense, she'd jumped out of the frying pan and into the fire. She leaned back, considering. So, she'd had six wonderful weeks before the bottom dropped out of her world. She'd found peace and lost it. Before she could decide what to do next, she had to find peace again.

Home beckoned, not Chicago, but the little girl comfort of her mother's arms to help soothe the pain. She chewed her knuckles thoughtfully, then stood, filled with new resolve.

"Where did I put those suitcases?" she muttered as she tapped the countertop thoughtfully, then smiled in triumph. Where else but in the attic with everything else the Neills had decided they didn't need over the course of the last hundred years?

Her gaze focused on the diaries. She hesitated, tempted to thumb through them. Or maybe she should take them with her.

No, she decided instantly. It was better to leave well enough alone. A trip through the old man's memory lane might bring on another crying jag, and she already had a headache from the last one. She gathered up the stack and headed for the attic, first to stow the volumes where they belonged, and next to find her suitcases.

Half an hour later, she'd searched half the attic, but the suitcases remained lost in the clutter of the huge, open space. She ran a hand through her hair and groaned when her fingers displaced a dusty cobweb.

"No question where I picked up that," she said. "Somebody ought to clean this place up." More than a hundred years of dust and junk had accumulated up here. She still found it amazing that Sam's and Ben's busy fingers hadn't sorted and catalogued it.

Her glance fell on the diaries again, resting on top of a stack of boxes she'd already moved twice in her search. Then she turned away, forcing her thoughts elsewhere. She didn't need to read them to know Sam thought they supported his argument. But he still refused to face the facts.

Frowning, she returned to her search. As she worked, she considered what to do about the new job, the one they were supposed to celebrate last night. She'd agreed to start in two weeks. She could always tell them she'd changed her mind and return to Chicago. She had friends there. She hadn't had time to make more than casual acquaintances here, except for Sam.

But that would be running away. She'd done that once this summer and look where it had landed her. Plus, there was Kyle to consider. She couldn't just sneak into town without his knowing it, not unless she avoided all their friends. She couldn't face his I-told-you-so or, worse yet, his renewed pursuit. He would pursue, she was sure, even if only to assuage his damaged ego.

Two weeks was long enough to put her life in perspective. If she wasn't comfortable living near Sam when she returned to Kansas City, she could always take an apartment closer to her job until she could face him or she sold Neill House.

She shoved another box aside. Her glance strayed to the diaries again. She sighed. No matter what she did, they piqued her curiosity.

Finally, she could stand it no longer. She opened the oldest, most tattered of the journals. She skimmed through the years, through that book and the next and the next after that. She turned some pages quickly and lingered over others until she reached the part about Sarah's growing up years in this house.

She'd been the perfect child, even if her grandfather wrote that as she grew older she seemed too uncaring of practical matters to survive on her own. Great Uncle Ben thought Sam would be her buffer between reality and the gentler, dreamier world she occupied. He failed to see how mismatched they were until it was too late. The marriage was foundering when Sarah and her parents were killed.

Later entries catalogued Sam's contributions to the restoration of Neill House. They also reflected the growing closeness between the two men as they exorcised their mutual grief, as well as Sam's guilt. Ben blamed his granddaughter for that, for running away from her problems instead of working them out. If she'd stayed that night, she wouldn't have been killed in the furnace explosion. And Sam's guilt wouldn't exist. In the end, Hilary thought, Sam was Uncle Ben's family. Yet Ben left the house to his brother, and thus to Hilary, because blood ties were strongest. Perhaps Uncle Ben had realized what Hilary had forgotten in her own weak pride. Sam *had* moved on with his life. He didn't need Neill House or memories of Sarah. The house wasn't the symbol Hilary thought it was. Neither were the pearls, she realized.

The old man's final memories of Sarah, scattered through the last few entries, struck Hilary the hardest. Through Great Uncle Ben's words, she began to understand the shy, sensitive woman she'd never met. She realized that even at the funeral, Sam's guilt outweighed his grief. Sarah had haunted him, only not the way Hilary had assumed.

Hilary wiped away her tears and stood, stretching stiff muscles. Glancing out the window, she noticed the sun's angle had shifted drastically, that it was now well into the afternoon. For the first time in hours, she noticed the heat that made her sweaty shirt stick to her back. She pulled the shirt out, fanning herself with the tail. It had to be over a hundred degrees up here. Judging from the angle of light shining through the west window, it was afternoon now.

Hilary grabbed the diaries and hurried down the stairs. The comparative coolness of the lower level of the house hit her like a blast of air conditioning. The sensation registered, but she didn't take time to enjoy it or shower away the stickiness. She had to talk to Sam.

She dialed Sam's number from the upstairs study, then let the phone ring twenty times before hanging up. Thinking he might be working outdoors, she jogged over to his house. His truck was gone. She checked indoors and out anyway, wondering whether she should wait until he returned or just go back home. Then she checked the calendar. It was Thursday. He had an afternoon class.

She sank onto the floor and tried to think.

How could she retrieve what she'd thrown away? He might take her back, but he would have doubts, reservations about her lack of trust in him.

*   *   *

The bright red flag on the mailbox reflected in the headlights on Sam's truck as he rounded the last curve. He frowned. The mailman must have forgotten to put it down when he'd picked up the bills Sam left this morning. Or maybe he'd skipped Sam's place again. The regular guy did that sometimes when there was only junk mail to deliver and traffic was bad on this curve. Usually Sam didn't mind, but it seemed everything irritated him tonight.

When he pulled up next to the box, though, he saw something no mailman in his right mind would have left. A wisp of red satin and black lace waved in the wind for all the world to see.

"What the heck is that thing?"

It couldn't be what it looked like. He pulled into the driveway, stopping barely off the road. He jammed the gears into park. Leaping from the truck, he hopped over the ditch and untangled the elastic edging from the flag.

A pair of women's underwear. A very scanty, very sexy pair. It had to be some kind of prank. Or . . .

He turned, staring thoughtfully across the road. Hilary wouldn't have done something like this. She didn't own anything like this. His chin came up sharply. She might. What did he *really* know of the woman?

He frowned. Maybe she'd worn stuff like this before him. Or maybe it was a joke played by one of his more daring students.

He jerked open the mailbox, looking for a note. He found junk mail, bills, and a matching bra—if two see-through triangles of fabric and a bit of elastic could qualify as that particular item of clothing.

He stared across the road, considering. A length of cloth flapped from a fencepost beyond the opened gate. The pale color caught the light of the dusk-to-dawn bulb at the edge of his yard. A memory of peach satin flashed through his mind, bringing a soft smile to his lips. Hilary had done this.

He started across the road, then jumped back as a horn blared, and a battered white truck whooshed past him. The truck screeched to a halt, backed up and stopped, the driver's window even with Sam.

Randy the plumber spat tobacco juice on the asphalt next to Sam's feet. "You all right? You stepped right out there like you didn't even see the lights comin' your way."

"Sorry, I had something on my mind." Sam stuffed the red bits of satin and lace into a back pocket and willed the man to go away.

"The wife mailed the estimate this morning. If I'd known I'd be running into you—no pun intended—well, I would have just hand-delivered it," Randy said, then hesitated. "You sure you're all right?"

Sam nodded distractedly. The peach nightgown, at least he thought that's what it was, waved in the wind more blatantly than the underpants had. He prayed Randy wouldn't look in that direction.

"I'm fine, just in a bit of a hurry," Sam said, backing toward his truck. "I have an appointment later."

Randy nodded. "You just give me a call." He smiled and checked in the mirrors. As the truck wheels began to roll, Randy glanced the wrong way. The truck stopped. His head swiveled on his stocky neck from the flapping silk to Sam, his eyes squinted in a puzzled frown. Sam felt the heat creep up his neck and suffuse his face, giving away too much. A broad smile split Randy's face.

"You have a nice evenin', sir."

"Bye, Randy," Sam managed in a slightly strangled voice. Heaven help them all when this story started circulating around the neighborhood. He was simply grateful the man didn't ask what it all meant. He didn't know yet himself. It could mean she'd read the diaries and changed her mind about him. Or it could be an elaborate kiss-off from a very angry woman. But that sobering thought didn't slow his heart rate to a normal beat.

He waited until Randy's truck disappeared around the bend, then hurried across the road. His eyes confirmed what his instincts already knew. There was no mistaking whose gag this was. It was the same peach gown he'd swiped from Hilary the night her ex-fiancé had arrived. Once the ex was gone, he'd confessed and told her where he'd hidden it.

He carefully untangled the gown's hem from the wire, then strolled fifty feet or so up Hilary's driveway to retrieve the matching robe. On the latch of the second gate was a hot-pink teddy. His already overactive imagination went wild as he pictured Hilary's body inside the teddy, then sliding out of it.

A black garter dangled from a spent daylily stem on the other side of the gate. His heart rate raced. He'd never have guessed the woman owned such things.

Every light in the house blazed, as did all the outdoor fixtures. It was nearly bright enough in her yard to read small print. Another robe, this one hot pink like the teddy, was draped over the snowball bush near the house. He followed a trail of barely-there panties to the backyard, where the trail ended. He glanced around, searching for the next silken clue, but saw nothing.

He started for the back porch at a lope, then sidestepped to the water spigot at the corner of the house. Another of those scanty bras was tied around the handle.

He didn't need to look further or to follow the zigzagged lengths of hose across the yard to see where they finally ended.

Smiling, he headed toward the cluster of forsythia

bushes where he first watched her dance in the moonlight. He slowed, catching his breath as he spotted her sitting in the grass as if she'd been waiting for him. The barn light cast a golden path that ended just beyond her.

He slowed, confused at her appearance. After the seductive trail he'd followed, he expected to find her in another such delectable bit of nothing, or maybe just nothing.

Except for her hair, which she'd left uncovered, she looked as if she'd stepped out of a nineteenth century daguerreotype. She stood at his approach, brushing the grass from the heavy brown skirt, the one she'd borrowed to wear at the park. The coarse cotton blouse was loosely tied at the neckline, exposing the creamy skin and a single strand of pearls.

The Neill pearls.

He stopped in the shadows beyond the trail of light. "What are these for?" he asked, holding up the armful of lingerie he'd gathered.

"To get your attention. I wasn't sure you'd speak to me after the things I said."

"If I felt that way, I wouldn't be here now," he answered.

She reached out, lifting the smaller items from the pile. "These are my dreams and my fantasies. They all belong to you now." He saw in her shaking hands how uncertain she was, how much of her soul she was risking.

"And this?" He held up the peach gown.

"I bought that as a promise to be true to myself and do what's best for me, whether it meant being alone or being with someone. I want to be with you."

Sam caressed her cheek with the back of his hand while he tried to find his voice. "Am I what's best for you?" For the first time he wasn't so certain. Look what he'd brought her to; he didn't want to see her level her pride. But that's what she was doing.

She touched the pearls. "This is my heritage and my trust." She didn't explain the clothes. She didn't need to. His memory and instincts filled in the blanks.

"You did all of this for me?" Such trite, inane words, he thought and tried for something better. "I only wanted you to believe me. But this, well, it's completely unexpected. Like you."

"Forgive me?" She faced him, meeting his gaze uncertainly. "I should have listened. I should have trusted you." She wasn't pleading, but offering peace, a new beginning. A very extravagant, very sexy beginning, judging from the presentation so far.

"I'm the one who's sorry. I should have explained about Sarah," he said.

She shook her head. "You offered me the diaries weeks ago. If I'd read them then, I wouldn't have jumped to certain conclusions."

She stepped closer, touching gentle fingers to his lips. "Can we start over?"

He shook his head, folding her into his arms before her disappointment could fully register across her features. "It's too late to start over. I want to pick up where we left off."

She laughed in relief. "Me, too. Marry me."

"That's my line," he protested, though not too seriously. He was more interested in kissing her, in reassuring himself that it was really her and not just some fantasy he'd conjured up from his dreams.

She allowed him one kiss, one long, lingering kiss that healed more than any words could. "You proposed last time. It's my turn," she insisted.

"Name the date," he said, stepping into the light and taking her with him.

She laughed, letting the wild, free sound bubble

around them. She slipped from his arms, dancing in a joyous circle and eluding his grasp.

"Come back here," he called when she disappeared behind the forsythia.

The heavy skirt floated over the shrub, landing on his shoulder. The blouse didn't sail nearly so well and caught on a twig near the top of a bush. Then he heard the gentle hiss of the hose nozzle.

He stepped around the bush into the spray of warm water showering down from the crook of the tree.

"Sam, your clothes!"

He held his arms wide in invitation. With a slow, positively naughty grin, she stepped forward and nimbly slipped the buttons through their holes in spite of the damp fabric. Talented fingers, he reminded himself. Skilled enough to keep him fascinated for a lifetime.

The twinkling drops of water danced through the dim light like tiny stars to land on her skin. His mouth grew dry, just watching the glistening trails that streamed gently down her neck, over the soft planes of her shoulders, and down lower to drip from the rosy tips of her breasts. And he couldn't resist the lure of those trails as his water nymph danced into his arms and away again. He had to touch her, kiss her, taste the sweetness that was her.

He sobered as she touched his flesh, fumbled with his belt, and somehow managed to unbuckle it. He realized then that fumbling in the darkness was not the way they should begin anew. He lifted her into his arms and headed for the house with long, distance-eating strides.

"What are you doing?"

"Hunting for a bed, woman."

She sighed. "Haven't you ever made love outdoors, Sam?"

"Mosquitoes," he reminded her. He sidetracked to turn off the hose, putting her down while he twisted the knob. While his back was turned, the gray-eyed witch slipped away from him.

He chased her through the house, up the stairs and down the hall to the big east bedroom with its wide, four-poster bed.

She reached for the light switch, but he stopped her.

"I need to see you tonight. Not just your body, but your eyes. They are the mirrors of your soul, and I need to believe you're really mine now," he said, baring his own soul to this woman, his mate.

She nodded. "We're partners," she whispered. "My strengths will complement yours, and between us there are no weaknesses."

Sam smiled. "Don't ever stop loving me, Hilary Neill."

"Never," she promised.